6

W10

R 2017
017

)17

'If I ever get married, I want it to be here on the riverbank where I make my vows.'

Luke raised his eyebrows.

'If you ever get married…?'

They were on a delicate subject, Megan thought uneasily. Both were eager to know each other better, and if she spoke the truth it could bring an end to that.

'I would want to be the first love of the man I married.'

'I see,' Luke said flatly. 'No one could blame you for that.'

But *he* didn't have that right. He'd forfeited it because of one big mistake.

He supposed he should be thankful for the straight talk and put those sorts of thoughts out of his mind.

But was that possible?

Abigail Gordon loves to write about the fascinating combination of medicine and romance from her home in a Cheshire village. She is active in local affairs, and is even called upon to write the script for the annual village pantomime! Her eldest son is a hospital manager, and helps with all her medical research. As part of a close-knit family, she treasures having two of her sons living close by, and the third one not too far away. This also gives her the added pleasure of being able to watch her delightful grandchildren growing up.

Recent titles by the same author:

CITY DOCTOR, COUNTRY BRIDE
THE VILLAGE DOCTOR'S MARRIAGE
COMING BACK FOR HIS BRIDE
A FRENCH DOCTOR AT ABBEYFIELDS

A WEDDING
IN THE VILLAGE

BY
ABIGAIL GORDON

MILLS & BOON®
Pure reading pleasure

First published in Great Britain 2007
Large Print edition 2008
Harlequin Mills & Boon Limited,
Eton House, 18-24 Paradise Road,
Richmond, Surrey TW9 1SR

ISBN: 978 0 263 19927 7

Set in Times Roman 17 on 19¾ pt.
17-0108-52308

Printed and bound in Great Britain
by Antony Rowe Ltd, Chippenham, Wiltshire

A WEDDING
IN THE VILLAGE

For Roger, who is a tower of strength.

CHAPTER ONE

MEGAN MARSHALL was smiling as the train pulled into the small country station.

She was home and happy to be so, and as Mike from the ticket office came hurrying forward to help her lift her cases out on to the platform, it was as if the two weeks she'd just spent in Florida belonged to another life.

A life in which she'd laughed a lot, played a lot, flirted a bit, and in which the two friends she'd gone with hadn't guessed that underneath her carefree manner there had been worry.

She was soon going to be facing a big responsibility and was concerned in case she wouldn't be up to it. There were going to be changes in the medical practice in the beautiful Cheshire village where she lived, and she was going to be very much involved in them.

They were connected with her parents, Margaret and James Marshall, both GPs, who had worked there side by side for as long as she could remember.

But now retirement was on the cards and arrangements were having to be made regarding the practice and who would be taking over. It was a problem that was half-solved as Megan had followed in their footsteps by going into medicine.

Since her degree she'd been hospital-based, but not now. That had changed. She'd been brought up around the village practice, played at doctors and nurses there when she had been small and, not wanting it to go out of the family, had taken GP training so that her presence might fill some of the gap that her parents were going to leave.

She wasn't going to be doing it on her own. Another GP was needed. An experienced doctor who would help her to offer the standard of care that had always been present there.

Her parents were at the surgery now, making the final choice out of three applicants. When she'd got off the airport train in Manchester, Megan had phoned them to say that she would be catching the local train shortly and would one of them meet her at the station?

'That could be difficult,' her mother had said. 'We're in the middle of the final interviews. I'll ask Henry to pick you up in his taxi, Megan. It's lovely to know you're back. Are you coming straight here? If you do, you'll be able to meet the person you're going to be spending a lot of time with in the future We're pretty sure who it's going to be. He stands out way above the others. You'll be fortunate to have him working beside you in our small rural backwater.'

'All right. I'll come straight there,' Megan said, thinking that although she couldn't wait to get back to her little cottage on the hillside, she may as well get it over and done with.

'Been away to get your strength up before your parents leave, have you, Megan,' Henry Tichfield, the local taxi driver, asked as he piled her luggage into the boot.

She smiled. 'Something like that, Henry.

Heaven knows when I'll get the chance for another holiday.'

It was the lunch-hour, one of the quietest times in the surgery. The morning patients had been seen, the house calls done, and there would be a lull until the later surgery in the afternoon.

Megan could hear voices coming from the office up above, but the door was closed so she went and made a mug of coffee and chatted to the receptionist who was covering the lunch-hour.

When she heard footsteps on the stairs she felt her mouth go dry. The moment she'd been dreading had come. Since she'd joined the practice there had always been her parents to go to with any problems, but soon all that would be changed. She was going to be in close contact with a stranger every minute of her working day.

'Ah! There you are, Megan. Just at the right moment for introductions,' her mother was saying as she led the way down the stairs, with the new doctor behind her and her father bringing up the rear.

When she raised her head with a weak smile

on her face it froze, and a voice that she'd never expected to hear again exclaimed, 'But of course! Megan! Megan Marshall. Your first name hasn't been mentioned. Otherwise it might have registered that we already know each other.'

'That's great news!' her father cried. 'It will make everything so much easier when you take over, Luke.'

I wouldn't bank on that, she thought numbly.

Luke Anderson had been one of the tutors in her last year at university and with his dark good looks and lean masculine appeal he'd been a target for every romantically inclined female on the campus, including herself.

Incredibly, he hadn't been married or in any sort of relationship. It had also seemed that was how he had wanted it to stay, as no amount of feminine wiles from some of the most ravishing of his students had got them anywhere. The impression he had given was that he had been doing a job he'd liked and his only interest in those in his classes had been a desire to see they did well in their finals.

Even so, she'd sent him a Valentine card, along with all the other hopefuls, and he must have recognised her handwriting as the next time she'd been at one of his lectures he'd called her back at the end of it and said with a glint in his eye that could have meant anything, 'Roses are not always red, Megan, and I would describe the colour of violets as deep purple.' With that he'd left her standing alone in the lecture hall with a face red as the roses he'd referred to.

She'd discovered afterwards that he'd made no comments to anyone else who'd sent him a card and wondered why he'd singled her out. One thing had been sure, she wasn't going to ask him. The embarrassment of those moments in the lecture hall had not been forgotten quickly, but once she'd got her degree and gone into hospital work it had been pushed to the back of her mind.

For the last three years she'd been a junior doctor on the wards, until her parents had dropped their bombshell regarding retirement and a house they were contemplating buying in Spain.

Luke Anderson was smiling and holding out his hand as he spoke, and as she shook it Megan managed to resurrect her grimace of before.

'Luke was one of my tutors at college,' she told her parents. 'This is the last place I would ever have expected to see him.'

'I've actually come to live in the village,' he said, and her discomfort increased. 'I'm going to be staying with my sister who lives at Woodcote House.'

Megan could actually feel her jaw dropping. 'Are you saying that Sue Standish is your sister?'

'Yes.'

'She never said.'

'Sue doesn't know we knew each other.'

'We were just as surprised as you when we heard that Luke was related to Sue,' her mother said. 'We've known her a long time, haven't we, James, and she and Megan are good friends. We were all so sorry when Gareth died so suddenly.'

'That's why I'm here,' he said sombrely. 'To give a hand with the boys and offer any other support she might need. I'm going to stay with Sue for as long as she needs me, and then find a place of my own in the village.'

This was turning out to be more disturbing by the minute, Megan was thinking. Luke Anderson was back in her life with a vengeance, and to top it all he was going to be living with Sue and the children. Why hadn't her friend said?

She'd intended being in on the interviewing and was wishing now that she had been, but when two school friends had asked her to go to Florida with them for a couple of weeks, her mother had said, 'You must go, Megan. It could be a long time before you get another break once we've gone.'

So she'd let herself be persuaded, knowing that whatever decision her parents came to, they would have her best interests at heart while sorting out the future of the practice.

She hadn't thought about Luke Anderson in a long time and supposed that the rest of the girls attending his classes hadn't either. Once they'd all got their degrees they'd been off to pastures

new, faces that he too would soon have forgotten.

If it hadn't been for the Valentine card incident
she might have been pleased to see him, but as
the memory of it came back all she could think
of was what a fool she'd made of herself then.

She'd avoided him like the plague afterwards
and had caught him observing her thoughtfully
a couple of times, and that had been it.

'I was in general practice before I took up
lecturing,' he said easily, as if quite unaware of
her confusion. 'So I'm hoping I won't be *too*
rusty. When I heard from Sue that there was a
vacancy here, it seemed heaven sent. A job that
was virtually on her doorstep.'

'So you're not lecturing any more.'

'No. I was ready for a change in any case. I'm
looking forward to a spell of village life,
having always been city-based and now, if you
will excuse me, I'll pop round to tell Sue and
the boys my good news.'

'He'll be joining the practice in a month's
time,' her father said after Luke had gone

striding down the street to where Woodcote House stood back from the road on a sizeable plot. 'And I have to take my hat off to him, leaving a job at the university for the life of a country GP so he can give his sister some support.

'But your mother and I need to know if *you're* happy about the arrangement, Megan. You're the one who will be working with him every day. How do you feel about it?'

It wasn't an easy question to answer. Maybe in a couple of days' time she might be able to come up with a truthful reply, but she was still dazed by the unexpected meeting and the effect that seeing him again was having on her.

She'd forgotten how gorgeous he was. Time had dimmed the memory of his attractions, but they were still there. The dark-haired, dark-eyed, clean-cut image of him.

If it hadn't been for the stupid Valentine card and his cool remarks when he'd let her know he'd known who'd sent it, she would have been pleased to be meeting up with him again.

Instead, she was going to be nervous and constrained when he came to join the practice.

Her father was still waiting for an answer to his question and, not wanting to put the blight on their plans, she gave him a hug and told him, 'It's fine by me. I'm just getting used to the shock of seeing him and knowing that we're going to be working together. I don't remember seeing him at the funeral, which is strange if he's Sue's brother.'

'That's because he wasn't there. He was in hospital, recovering from the effects of a car crash, and they wouldn't allow him out.'

A few days later, Megan went to see Sue. They chatted for a while, and then Megan gently asked why she'd never mentioned that Luke Anderson was her brother. Sue observed her with lacklustre eyes and said, 'I didn't know that you knew him, Meg, otherwise I would have told you.'

Sue and Gareth had run a profitable garden centre on land at the back of their house before he'd died from a sudden heart attack. Since then she'd been trying to cope with the business and two boys who were being difficult and unruly since they'd lost their dad.

Although Sue had been delighted to see Megan and catch up, she looked tired and drained.

'Luke has been fantastic,' Sue said. 'Having him here will make all the difference. For one thing the boys dote on him and will take note of what he says.'

'He wasn't at the funeral, was he?' asked Megan.

'No. He was in hospital, recovering from a car crash. But once he was discharged he was on my case. Sorting me out. Stopping me from going crazy.'

'Has he no family of his own?'

Sue shook her head. 'He was married once but it didn't work out and you know what they say about once bitten.'

'So when is he moving in?'

'Soon. He has an apartment near the university and is sorting out all the loose ends connected with that and the job. I imagine that he'll move in here the weekend before he becomes part of the practice. You'll like him, Megan. He's great.'

'Mmm, I'm sure I will,' Megan said, trying to sound confident. "It's going to be changes all round, isn't it?"

'Yes, it is,' Sue agreed bleakly, and Megan thought that what was happening in her friend's life made her own misgivings seem as nothing.

As she waited for Luke to arrive in the village Megan kept pondering over what Sue had said. That he'd been married once and it hadn't worked out. Each time she thought about it she shuddered. Suppose he'd been married at the time she'd sent the Valentine card? He'd commented about roses being red and violets blue, but had had nothing to say about the rest of it, where she'd written, 'And I have to admit I'm attracted to you.' If he had been married at the time, he must have felt she'd had some cheek.

Another thought that kept haunting her was that she was happy working in the village practice. It had been part of her life as long as she could remember and she was apprehensive at the thought of someone who'd once been her dream man taking her parents' place in her working life.

Why couldn't he have been satisfied with running the market garden for Sue instead of applying for the vacancy in the practice? But even as she asked herself the question, the answer was there. Sue had her own staff to do that, village folk, long tried and tested. His function would most likely be the admin of the business, rather than nurturing seedlings and selling bedding plants, conifers and suchlike.

The two boys, Owen and Oliver, would be the biggest problem. They might have coped better with losing their father if they'd had some warning, but he'd been gone in seconds and they were lost without him. It would be a stroke of genius on their uncle's part if he could bring them through such a terrible time, unscarred and well adjusted.

After seeing her parents off at the airport on a Sunday afternoon a month later, Megan returned to her cottage in sombre mood. For once the charm of the small stone house in its beautiful setting didn't register.

The sign over the door said MEGAN'S PLACE, and that was what it was.

Everything inside it had been chosen carefully by her. Furniture, curtains, carpets, the lot, and every blade of grass in the small lawn outside was lovingly tended by her, but not today.

Life was changing. Her mum and dad had gone. She would be out on a limb from now on, and sitting on an opposite branch would be the man she'd once told she was attracted to him.

She could see Woodcote House from her back bedroom window and as she gazed downwards a big black car pulled into the drive, and in the same second Sue and the boys appeared in the doorway.

So he hadn't changed his mind, she thought. The die was cast.

After she'd eaten Megan went to sit on a small terrace at the back of the cottage and watched the sun go down. It was a warm summer evening with the scent of flowers on the air. Lots of people would be out and about, in The Badger, the village pub, down by the river, or going more upmarket and dining at Beresford Lodge, a hotel just outside the village. While here *she* was, feeling lost and lonely with no inclination to do anything other than sit and mope.

Lost in her thoughts, she wasn't aware of time passing until she heard the front gate click and sat upright. It was strange for someone to call at this hour. There was silence for a few seconds and then she heard footsteps on the stone path leading from the front of the cottage.

When he appeared he was silhouetted against the setting sun, but she could tell by his height and the trim build of him that it was the man who hadn't been out of her thoughts since the day her parents had presented the new doctor to her.

As she rose to her feet he took a step forward and she saw that he was carrying a bottle of wine and smiling, and she wished she'd stayed seated as her legs felt weak.

'How did you know where to find me?' she asked in a voice that didn't sound like hers, and knew it was a stupid question. Sue would have told him.

'It wasn't hard,' he said. 'Megan Marshall, the village doctor, is a household name. Actually, it was Sue who pointed me in the right direction. She's in the middle of making a meal and after we've eaten the boys are going to show me around the place so that I can get my bearings for tomorrow.

'But first I felt I wanted to see you. We only met briefly that day at the surgery and I got the impression that it was something of a shock and that you weren't over the moon about it. So I've come to suggest that we drink a toast to our future relationship as village GPs. If that's all right with you. I've also come…'

Here we go, she thought, stifling a groan. He's going to mention the Valentine card. Wants to wipe the slate clean before we go any further. I wish the ground would open up and swallow me.

'Because I thought you might be feeling a bit

low after your parents' departure,' he was saying, and her eyes widened. 'Also, I feel I should tell you that I won't be pulling rank or anything like that. I will be relying on you to put me right if I make any mistakes.'

He'd come to sit on the seat beside her, still with the bottle in his hand, and she said in a low voice, 'And is that it?'

He smiled. 'Yes. I think so. I can't think of anything else. So, are we going to drink a toast, Megan?'

She nodded, speechless with relief, and went inside to get a bottle opener and glasses. By the time she'd done that she'd found her voice and, standing in the kitchen doorway, she said, 'Shall we drink it inside or out?'

He got to his feet. 'Inside would be nice. I'd love to see what your home is like. It's a beautiful place you have here.'

'*I* think so,' she said stiffly, still on edge, and stepped back to let him in. 'Do make yourself comfortable. Though perhaps you should pour the wine first, as you've brought it.'

'Whatever,' he said easily and did as she'd

suggested. 'To us, Megan,' he said, raising his glass. 'To a good working partnership.'

As he took a sip of his wine, Luke wondered if she remembered sending him the Valentine card. When he'd behaved like a moron and left her red with embarrassment, instead of telling her why he hadn't been ready to take her up on it. She had been the only one of his students that he'd ever taken note of. Small, dainty, with red-gold hair and green eyes, she'd moved like a dream.

But it hadn't just been those things that had caught his attention. It had been the way she'd worked, steadily and with zeal, while some of the students had thought that university was a big joke. An opportunity to waste their parents' money on living it up.

There had been a strange irony in discovering that half the class fancied him, including the girl sitting opposite him, when his marriage had crashed and he had been going through a bitter divorce.

He checked the time. 'I must go, Megan. Sue will have the meal ready by now, and the boys will be raring to spend some time with me, as

I'm the nearest thing they're going to get to a dad.'

He sighed. 'The poor kids are in a state at losing him, which is only natural. It's the first time they've been this close to death, and are striking out against it in the only way they know how. They desperately want a father figure at the moment and I'm going to be there for them for as long as they need me. That applies to Sue as well. She'll be all right when they are. So it's going to be taking one day at a time.'

'They're fortunate to have you looking out for them,' Megan said awkwardly.

He shrugged. 'I just wish I could have been here sooner. Anyway, I really must go. It's been a pleasant evening, Megan, so thank you.'

As Megan showed him out, he paused in the doorway. 'How long have you lived here?'

Megan shrugged. 'Only a short time. When I knew that Mum and Dad were leaving the area I didn't want to be living on my own in their house. It would have been too big for me. So I bought this place.'

'A good choice,' he said, and strode down the path. When he reached the gate he raised his hand in a brief salute and then drove off.

When he'd disappeared from sight Megan let out a deep breath and went back inside. He was the last person she'd expected to see appearing out of the summer dusk. It had been a nice gesture to suggest a toast, and an exquisite relief not to have been reminded of her youthful crush. Maybe he'd forgotten. If he had she would send up a prayer of thanks. But how was she to know? It could be that he remembered it very well and was saving the mention of it for a later date.

Nevertheless she went to bed in a happier frame of mind than she'd been in all day and it was due to Luke Anderson.

The house was still. Sue had gone to bed early with a headache and the boys were also asleep. They'd been great while they'd been showing him around the village, but at bedtime Oliver, who was eleven years old, had been awkward.

He'd wanted to stay up and watch television

and wouldn't get undressed until Luke had told him he had to as it was school in the morning, and on *no* account was he to disturb his mother. He'd done as he'd been told but with a scowl on his face. When Luke had gone to check on them, Owen, the thirteen-year-old had been fast asleep, and Oliver thankfully had been on the point of dozing off.

He'd gone to bed himself then and as he lay thinking about the day, the short time he'd spent with Megan was at the forefront of his mind. When they'd met a month ago at the practice he'd been as dumbfounded as she had been at meeting up again and in such circumstances.

When she'd sent him the Valentine card he'd been at his lowest ebb. His marriage to Alexis had just ended in divorce. He'd been feeling angry and betrayed. And even if Megan hadn't been his student, the thought of another relationship hadn't been bearable.

Since his marriage had ended, he hadn't looked at another woman, and it might have stayed that way if he hadn't met Megan again.

But again the time wasn't right. Then he'd been reeling from his divorce, and now he had his hands full with a distraught mother and her fatherless sons.

As a reminder of that fact he heard the creak of a bedroom window being opened in the next room to his, and when he went to investigate he found Oliver halfway out of the window and preparing to jump onto the roof of an outhouse down below.

When he saw him he hesitated and Luke said, 'Don't even think of it, Oliver.' And taking his arm, he helped him back into the room.

'Where were you intending going?' he asked quietly, dreading that he'd been on the point of running away.

'Mothing,' was the surly reply. 'I meet my friend Mikey out on the lane at the back and we go into the fields with our nets.'

'And does your mother know?'

'No. She wouldn't let me if she knew.'

'I see,' Luke said unsmilingly. 'So how about we do a deal. If you promise to go back to bed and stay there, I'll come with you and Mikey tomorrow night, and any other night for that matter, but you have to promise that you won't sneak out again.'

'What? You'll come mothing with us, Uncle Luke?' Oliver exclaimed with his good humour restored in the form of a wide smile. 'I didn't think grown-ups did that sort of thing.'

'They don't,' Luke told him dryly, 'but for you, Oliver, anything. And now I'm going to ring your friend's parents to tell them to check on his whereabouts.'

'He won't have gone out yet,' Oliver told him calmly. 'Mikey always waits until he hears me whistle beneath his window.'

'Is that so? Well, I'm going to phone them nevertheless, and now let's have you back in bed, Oliver. I have my first day at the surgery tomorrow and don't want to be half-asleep.'

'OK. I get the message.' Oliver grinned. 'Goodnight, Uncle Luke.'

When he looked in on him a few moments later Oliver wasn't pretending. He was fast asleep and as Luke closed the door quietly behind him, he decided that his own affairs were going to have to be put on hold for quite some time if tonight was anything to go by.

He'd taken on two big commitments, looking after his sister and her children, and the position at the practice, both requiring patience and stamina. Yet compared to living with Alexis they would seem like a holiday, and on that thought he turned on his side and slept.

CHAPTER TWO

WHEN Megan awoke the following morning the first thing that came to mind was Luke appearing in the sunset with a bottle of wine. Thinking about it, she wished she could have been a bit less stilted in her manner, but surprise and unease had been responsible for that.

And in the light of day the unease was back. She wasn't going to be able to cope with being on tenterhooks all the time in case the matter of the Valentine card came up, and she decided reluctantly that the best thing to do was take the bull by the horns and mention it herself.

That way it would be over and done with. She would be able to work alongside him more comfortably when she'd reassured him that the card had just been the result of a youthful crush. It was going to be the first thing she did when she got to the surgery, she decided. She would mention it casually, poking wry fun at herself, and it would be over.

She was using her mother's room for consultations and Connie, the cleaner, had been asked to come in over the weekend to give the room that had been her father's a good spring clean, ready for Luke's arrival.

Megan had to smile when she saw it. Everywhere was immaculate. Connie had even put flowers on the window-sill and a fresh box of tissues for any patient who might be distressed during a consultation. All it needed now was the arrival of its new occupant.

It was a quarter past eight. In fifteen minutes the wheels would start turning and another day at the Riverside Practice would begin. Luke needed to get a move on. She wanted to introduce him to the staff and put him in the picture as to how the surgery was run before he settled himself behind the desk in the room that had been prepared for him.

He arrived just before eight-thirty, looking nothing like the man who'd toasted their partnership the night before. There was a tightness around his mouth and his tie needed knotting into place.

'I am so sorry,' he gasped. 'I intended being here early, but while I was under the shower those lads started playing Sue up, and once I'd sorted them and they'd ambled off to school, she began to cry. I couldn't leave her in that state, so I hung on until she'd calmed down.'

He flashed a wry smile. 'Does it sound as if I'm whingeing? I'm sorry if it does. The process of helping them adjust to losing their dad is not going to be easy. I'll tell you later what Oliver got up to last night.'

She nodded and thought, So much for putting the Valentine episode to bed. It would have to wait.

'I'll introduce you to the staff first,' she told him, 'and then a quick run through procedures. I'm sure the patients won't mind waiting a few moments longer.'

There were three receptionists, all efficient middle aged women, and after they'd smiled their welcome, Megan took him into the nurse's room where Pat Howarth, heading for retirement and dreading it, ruled the roost. Working alongside her was Kath Storey, a young mother of two little girls, who showed a less dominant attitude towards staff and patients.

The practice manager was Anne Faulkner, a quiet woman with accountancy qualifications, who rented the apartment above the surgery.

Connie, the cleaner, was absent. After her labours over the weekend Megan had told her to take the day off.

While the introductions were being made Luke was pleasant and friendly, but he didn't miss a thing. He'd smiled when he saw the flowers on the window-sill and said, 'You didn't have to do that, Megan.'

'I didn't,' she told him. 'It was Connie, the cleaner. She came in over the weekend to make the place spick and span for you.'

'Really? That was very thoughtful. Was it her idea?'

'No, it was mine.' Connie wasn't going to get all the praise, she decided. 'How about I start morning surgery while you wander round and watch us in motion? Maybe you could have a word with Anne, the practice manager, who can answer any questions you might have on the admin side. Then when I've finished we could join up for the house calls.'

'Sure,' he said easily. 'Whatever you say. And I promise that by tomorrow I will be up to speed.'

'I'm sure you will,' she told him, and left him to it.

When they met up just before midday Megan said, 'I suggest that we do the visits together for a few days. It will give you the opportunity to find your way around and meet some of the people in the village.'

Megan was driving, and as they headed along quiet roads lined with old stone cottages, their gardens full of colour, she told him about their first patient. 'Our first stop today is going to be at the home of my aunt, Isabel Chambers. And I feel I must warn you that she has a sharp tongue and doesn't wrap up her words. She's in her early seventies and has diabetes. But she's a strong woman. She's been on her own since her husband died forty years ago. They never had any children.'

She turned right up a leafy lane. 'I call to see her every Monday, just to make sure that she's all right, and that nothing regarding her health is going haywire. It's the house next to the old water mill on Rabbit Lane. We'll be there in a moment.'

As they walked up the path that led to the front door of a large stone house Luke saw that it was unlatched and a voice called from inside, 'Come in. Megan.' It belonged to a small grey-haired woman sitting facing them in a rocking chair and as bright eyes looked him up and down she said, 'So you've brought the new doctor to see me, Megan.'

'Yes, I have, Aunt Izzy. This is Luke Anderson. He and I are going to be running the practice from now on.'

'I see,' she said, and held out her hand for him to shake. 'You look all right to me,' she told him, taking in the height of him, and added to Megan, 'But I can see you getting a crick in your neck having to keep looking up.'

'I'm sure we'll manage,' she said quickly, dreading what was coming next.

She had cause to. 'Have you brought a wife and some young 'uns with you?' she asked Luke, and he shook his head.

'I'm afraid not,' he told her. 'I've come to look after some young 'uns but they aren't mine.'

'Dr Anderson is related to Sue Standish,' Megan told her aunt. 'He's come to give her some support.'

'Hmm. I see,' she said, then turned her sharp eyes on Megan. 'And who's going to look after you, lass? I told your mother and father they'd no right leaving you like that.'

Concealing her mortification Megan said, 'I don't need minding, Aunt Izzy. I'm twenty-nine years old.'

'Maybe,' the old lady said crustily, 'but you've been left with the practice to see to *and* a stranger to deal with.'

Megan saw Luke turn away to hide a smile and thought, enough is enough. 'I've come to check on your health, Aunt Izzy,' she said firmly. 'So let's see what the diabetes has been up to.

I'm going to test your blood pressure, and see what your blood-glucose levels are. And while I'm here I'll have a quick look at your feet.'

'All right,' she agreed, 'but don't rush me. Go and take a walk round the garden while I take my shoes off.'

'I'm so sorry,' Megan told him as they stood among summer's flowers. 'Aunt Izzy means nothing by it, but her comments can be miscon-strued.'

'You mean like the one about the stranger who is going to be a millstone around your neck,' he said quizzically. 'I promise I won't be that. I'll have to see if I can dredge up some charm from somewhere to win her over.'

Megan looked away. Since they'd met up again she was seeing another side to the man who'd shown such scant interest in her Valentine card, and charm was high on the list as far as *she* was concerned.

When the weekly check-up was over and she'd assured her aunt that all was well, Isabel nodded and turned her attention to Luke.

'I hope you're going to fit in here,' she said

dubiously. 'You look more of a town dweller than a countryman.'

'I'm going to fit in, Mrs Chambers,' he told her firmly. 'Have no doubts about that.'

As Megan drove to their next call, with Aunt Izzy's comments ringing in her ears, she felt that a change of subject was required and said, 'So tell me what young Oliver was up to last night.'

'I caught him halfway out of his bedroom window at gone midnight, all set to meet his friend Mikey.'

'Oh, dear!'

'Yes, indeed,' he agreed.

'So what did you do?'

'Nipped his nocturnal activities in the bud by bringing him back inside and making a deal with him.'

'What sort of a deal?'

'I promised I would go mothing with them tonight, as that's what they were intending doing.'

She was laughing. 'Ooh! That sounds exciting. Catching moths in a net.'

He raised his eyebrows. 'It's a better scenario than the kid being out in the fields without supervision at dead of night, don't you think?'

She nodded, serious now. 'Yes, of course. Young ones never see danger, do they?'

'No, they don't. Can you imagine the state Sue would have been in this morning if she'd found his bed empty? Her nerves are in shreds as it is, and there's something else.'

His tone was warning her that it wasn't a minor matter and she said slowly, 'What is it?'

'Some friends who live in France have invited her and the boys to stay with them for a few weeks for a change of scene. She's dead keen to go, but it would mean taking Owen and Oliver out of school and these days parents are in big trouble if they do that.'

'Surely it wouldn't be frowned upon in the circumstances.'

'Maybe not, but the lads don't want to go, and in any case Sue doesn't want them missing school.'

She could guess what was coming next. 'So?'

'So I've told her to go and leave them with me.'

'And what did she say to that?'

'Jumped at the chance. It's just what the poor girl needs. To get away for a while without any worries regarding her children.'

'So she's going.'

'Hmm. She was checking flights when I came out.'

'Sue does realise that you being part of the practice is a big responsibility?'

'Yes. I'm sure she does.'

'And having those two mixed-up boys to look after on your own could be an even bigger one, and then there's the business.'

'Am I being told off?' he asked. 'You think I won't be pulling my weight at the practice.'

'No, of course not,' she assured him, a bit too hastily. 'It's just that I feel Sue could have waited a while. You've been in the village less than twenty-four hours.'

'I appreciate that the practice comes first with you,' he said, and now his tone was cool. 'But those kids didn't ask to lose their father and they are at a difficult age in any case. I thought you might have understood that.'

'Of course I understand,' she flared. 'But think about it. You've been part of the practice for just over two hours and all you've thought about are your family problems.'

'So maybe you should wait and see how I perform,' he suggested in the same cool tone.

'Maybe I should,' she told him, and as they did the rest of the house calls neither of them had any further comments to make.

When they'd finished and were driving back to the surgery, Megan broke the silence to ask, 'Do you want to stop off somewhere for a quick sandwich and a drink? There's The Badger in the village and a tearoom not far away.'

'I suggest we call in at the tearoom,' he replied. 'Doctors propping up the bar in the lunch-hour doesn't seem quite right, even if we are only drinking coffee.'

'Fine by me,' she said dismissively.

They ate in silence and when they'd finished and were back at the practice he said levelly, 'I'm ready to take my share of the afternoon surgery. If there's anything I'm not sure about regarding the way things are done, I'll ask.'

'Yes, do that,' she told him, and went in and closed her door.

This is dreadful, she thought. We haven't even got through Luke's first day at the practice and we're at loggerheads. No one was more sorry for Sue and the boys than herself, but was her friend being fair to him?

When she'd known Luke before it had been his looks and status that had attracted her, but since he'd arrived in the village she was seeing another side to him. He was compassionate and caring, and in consequence thought her to be only interested in her own affairs. He hadn't said it, yet she knew it was what he was thinking. But she was relying on him to help her run the practice. Would he always be there when he was needed if Sue went ahead with her plans?

'How did it go?' she asked when the late surgery was over.

'Just a couple of hitches,' he said calmly, 'but the receptionists sorted me out. There was no need to disturb you.'

She could feel herself getting rattled again at the display of cool competence. It would be interesting to see how alert the new doctor at the practice was when he'd been up half the night mothing, she thought as she drove homewards.

She made a meal of sorts, but left most of it uneaten as the day's events took over her mind. Luke was going to be a liability, she thought sombrely. He'd admitted that he'd taken the position in the practice to be near Sue and the boys and she'd seen nothing wrong in that.

But at that time she hadn't expected he was going to be left in sole charge of Owen, Oliver *and* the garden centre at the back of Woodcote House. Somebody was going to have to keep an eye on the business and he was the obvious choice, being family and already on the premises.

Where on his list of priorities was the Riverside Practice going to come? she wondered dismally. And where would *she* come? In spite of her annoyance at what she saw as being let down by him, the old attrac-

tion was still there and it wasn't going to
go away.

But it wasn't sexual chemistry that was her
main concern at that moment. Her parents had
left with an easy mind, believing that between
them the practice would be in safe hands, and
today had made her doubt if that was going to
be the case.

Megan wasn't the only one thinking sombre
thoughts about the day that was past. When
she'd left for home Luke had told the staff that
he would lock up, and when the place was
empty he went into his room and stood gazing
thoughtfully out of the window.

It was a fantastic view in anybody's book.
The peaks rising ruggedly in the distance, and
closer the quaint village street with shops that
made the uniformity of supermarkets seem
soulless and synthetic.

He could see Megan's point of view.
Understood that she felt he was going to be a
loose cannon instead of a reliable partner. Sue
going away for a prolonged holiday on her own

was something he hadn't bargained for, yet he could see the wisdom of it. As well as support, the boys needed a firm hand at the moment and she was not in a fit state to provide it, but he was.

As to the business, he would concern himself about that when he had to. At the moment it was running smoothly. The staff were loyal and ready to help the grieving young widow in any way they could.

His main concern now was to convince Megan that he wasn't going to let her down and after her annoyance of earlier in the day he suspected it wasn't going to be easy.

At almost the same time as the evening before, Megan heard footsteps on the flagging outside, but this time it wasn't just one pair of feet, there were others, and *she* wasn't out in the garden, watching the sunset. She was hunched on the sofa, staring into space.

A knock on the front door brought her to her feet and, putting the chain on, she opened it warily. Her eyes widened when she saw the trio standing in her porch. Oliver was smiling across at her with a boy she didn't know by his side, and standing behind them was Luke.

'We wondered if you'd like to join us,' he said. 'It's a lovely night, perfect for mothing.'

She had to laugh. If this was a peace offering, it was original.

'I might if you'll give me time to put on some sensible shoes and tell me what I have to do,' she told him.

'No problem,' he said equably. 'We'll wait by the gate. We've walked up across the fields and our trainers might be muddy.'

When she appeared minutes later in jeans and a white cotton shirt that would stand out in the darkness, Oliver produced a net for her. She observed it blankly and asked, 'So what do I do?'

'We catch the moths in the net,' he told her. 'There are lots of them flying around in the dark, and when we shine a torch they are attracted to the light.'

'And what then?'

'We keep them in a jam jar so they can't get away, but Uncle Luke says it's cruel. So we're going to let them go when we get home.'

'Right,' she said gravely, and saw Luke's teeth flash whitely as he smiled in the fading light.

'Are you sure you want to come, Dr Marshall?' Oliver's friend asked.

'Absolutely,' she assured him. The irritations of the day had disappeared when she'd seen Luke on her doorstep.

As they walked along behind the two boys he said in a low voice. 'Have you noted the time? Half past nine. No midnight excursions. It's part of the deal.'

'You seem to have Oliver eating out of your hand at the moment.'

'Yes, but will it last?' he said dryly.

They were out in the fields for an hour and although Megan didn't catch many moths it was nice to be with Luke again in the quiet night. She stumbled over a tree root and his hand came out to save her. His clasp on her arm was the first time he'd touched her and it felt good. Whether he was experiencing the same sensation she didn't know. He wasn't showing it if he was.

When they got back to Woodcote House it was time to release the fluttering prisoners from the jam jars and, as they flew off into the night, Megan said, 'I don't know how they survived without air.'

'They had air,' Oliver assured her. 'Mikey and me, we punched holes in the lids.'

The lights were on in the house and Luke said, 'Sue will still be up.' He sent a wary glance in her direction. 'She's busy packing. Do you want a word?'

'Yes, why not?' she said as all her forebodings came back to the surface, and they both went upstairs to Sue's room.

'So you are off to France, Luke tells me,' she said after the two women had greeted each other.

'Yes,' Sue replied, looking perkier than she'd been in weeks.

'And the boys aren't going with you?'

'No. I don't want them to miss school.'

'So you're leaving Luke to see to things while you're gone.'

'Yes. He says everything will be fine.'

'I'm sure he does.' She gave her friend a swift kiss on the cheek and said, 'Have a lovely time, Sue. Maybe when you come back you'll be a little nearer to facing a future without Gareth.'

Forlorn once again, Sue whispered, 'I hope so.'

Having looked uncomfortable while the conversation was taking place, Luke spoke into the silence that followed and said, 'I'll run you home, Megan.'

As he went to find his car keys Megan knew she couldn't leave Sue like this. Putting her arms around her, she said gently, 'It can only get better. You've been at rock bottom, the way now is upwards. I'll do what I can to help Luke while you're away.'

'So?' Luke said as he drove up the hill towards her cottage. 'Am I still in trouble now you know that Sue is definitely going to France?'

'I don't know,' she said. 'I really don't know. I was ashamed back there because I wasn't being as supportive as I should. Yet I still feel that you are letting me down by taking on this huge burden of responsibility.'

'So you feel that nothing has changed since our few heated words in the lunch-hour.'

'Yes and no. I've had a lovely time mothing with you and the boys, and presume you delayed telling me that Sue was almost ready to leave because you didn't want to spoil things.'

'Correct, and spoil things it has, hasn't it?'

She didn't reply to that. 'I can't think straight,' she said wearily as he pulled up in front of the cottage. 'I ought to be praising you for your kindness and tolerance instead of complaining, but I can't. I'll see you in the morning, Luke. Maybe tomorrow will be a better day.'

He quirked a dark eyebrow in her direction and commented wryly, 'It can hardly be worse, can it? I may as well tell you the whole thing where Sue is concerned. She's flying out of Manchester tomorrow at ten o'clock in the morning, and before you ask, no, I have not offered her a lift to the airport. A taxi will be picking her up. She needs to be there at least two hours before the flight, and if I took her it would make me late for morning surgery.'

'By all means feel free to let me know that

I'm selfish and opinionated,' she said tightly as she got out of the car. 'Goodnight, Luke.'

He did *not* want it to be like this, Luke thought grimly as he returned to Woodcote House. He wanted to get to know the student from way back, who was now a country GP. When he'd agreed to stay with his sister and keep an eye on the boys, the last thing he'd anticipated had been being left in complete charge of them *and* the business almost as soon as he'd arrived in the village.

He also hadn't expected that an old attraction was about to rekindle. Life with Alexis had made him loth to get involved in another relationship, but now he wasn't so sure.

Back at the cottage Megan was admitting to herself that part of her annoyance was pique, because in the kind of life that Luke was planning for himself in the weeks to come, there wasn't going to be much room for her.

He was there before her the next morning and she wondered if he was trying to prove a point.

'Did Sue get off all right?' she asked, making no comment on his early arrival.

'Yes. She'll be killing time at the airport by now, I would imagine.'

'And the boys?'

'Breakfasted and on their way to school, and if you're going to ask if I've washed the pots and made the beds, the answer is no. The breakfast things went into the dishwasher and, wait for it, I asked Sue to find me a cleaner and a house-keeper. So bedmaking will be part of her duties.

'She didn't tell me that she'd found me both, until late last night, and I did wish she'd mentioned it earlier. It would have made you feel less uncertain of me if you'd known, wouldn't it?'

'Yes, possibly,' she said flatly. 'Who are they?'

'I haven't met them yet, but the cleaner is Connie, and according to Sue she was grateful for the extra hours. The other person is someone called Rebekah Wainright. She'll be working from twelve until six each weekday. Hopefully she will be there when I get home this evening so that we can introduce ourselves. But the main thing is that she'll be around when

Oliver and Owen come home from school. The last thing those two young ones need at the present time is coming home to an empty house.'

'I know Rebekah Wainright,' Megan said. 'She's a friend of Aunt Izzy's, and a good soul. I'm glad for both our sakes that Sue sorted all that out before she left.'

It was another dawn, another day, she thought. If she'd known yesterday what he was telling her now, she wouldn't have got herself in such a state. Now it was her turn to make a peace offering and, smiling across at him, she said, 'Last night I told Sue I would do all I could to help while she was away, but I was in an awkward position, torn between my commitment to the practice and the problems of a friend. I hope you'll forgive me, Luke.'

'There's nothing to forgive,' he said quietly. 'I let my longing to make life easier for Sue and the boys make me forget what I'm here for. And with regard to that, Megan, ten minutes to go and it will be time for the Riverside Practice to swing into action.'

'How do you manage to be so good-humoured all the time?' she asked as she perched on the corner of her desk and flipped through the mail. He didn't answer and when she looked up his face was thoughtful.

'It's because I'm content, I suppose. I'm here in this beautiful place with those I care about. When we knew each other before I was not at my best. I was at the tail end of a divorce and disillusioned with womankind in general. But I'm over all that. Ready for new beginnings, and coming here is one of them.'

'I see. Was that why you took such a dim view of the Valentine I sent you?'

It was out, she thought. She'd done the thing she'd been dreading and was waiting to hear what he had to say.

He shook his head. 'It wasn't like that. My first reaction was amazement when I found it on my desk amongst an assortment of others. For a few seconds I was flattered, until it dawned on me that it might be a joke. I remember that I handled it badly.'

'They were all doing it,' she said hastily, 'and

I thought I'd join in. It was a stupid thing to do, I'm afraid.'

'Think no more of it. I'd forgotten it.'

It was a lie, of course. He hadn't forgotten it, or *her*. But she wasn't to know that and instead of being relieved to have cleared the air Megan was wishing she'd never mentioned it. She'd presented Luke with the opportunity to let her see she meant nothing in his scheme of things.

When she went to make a quick coffee before calling in her first patient, Megan saw Elise Edwards, who owned the village bakery, chatting to one of the receptionists.

'I'm here again, Megan,' she said, half laughing, half apologetic. 'I'm haunting this place, aren't I?'

She was a jolly, buxom woman in her mid-forties, who until recently had rarely been seen at the surgery, but that seemed to be changing. First there had been a diagnosis of rheumatoid arthritis that Elise could have done without. Then there'd been something suspect in the colon that had turned out to be benign, and as she wasn't due for a check-up, it seemed as if there might be something new for her to fret about.

'So you're down on my list for today,' she said, and Elise shook her head.

'I'm afraid not. You didn't have a free slot, so I'm seeing the new doctor. What's he like?' she asked Kathy, the receptionist.

'Very nice,' was Kathy's reply, and as Megan went into the small surgery kitchen to make the coffee, she thought that was putting it mildly.

The only snag was that so far, not having said a wrong word, Luke was making *her* seem like some sort of a control freak, and it was the last thing she wanted him to see her as.

CHAPTER THREE

'ELISE EDWARDS,' Luke said when the two doctors surfaced at the end of the morning.

'What about her?' Megan asked. 'I spoke to her earlier. She's been going through a rough patch healthwise. I hope it wasn't anything too serious.'

'It all depends on how one views that kind of thing at her age.'

'I'm not with you.'

'The lady is pregnant, Megan.'

Megan's jaw dropped. 'What?'

'Yes. And, needless to say, she is somewhat stunned.'

'I can imagine,' she said, shaking her head in amazement. 'How old is she?'

'Forty-six,' said Luke. 'She's done a test from the chemist and it has shown positive, but she just couldn't believe it, and came to the surgery for proof positive.'

'What actually was her reaction?'

'A mixture of things. Dismay, trepidation, embarrassment, and maybe just a tinge of excitement.'

'No mention of termination, then.'

'Not at this stage, though I believe she already has teenage girls.'

Megan nodded. 'Yes. Sophie and Claudia. Their reaction to the news could be interesting. When this kind of thing happens in families where there are older children, they are sometimes horrified. They see nothing wrong in it in anyone else, but not Mum and Dad. I wonder what Elise will do? She has rheumatoid arthritis, but it is under control, so that shouldn't cause any problems in its present state. She's also recently had a scare with a lump that proved to be benign, *and* she runs a business. The baker's just down the street. She might decide to sell up with a new baby on the way.'

'What does her husband do?' asked Luke.

'He's one of the gamekeepers at Lord

Marriott's place up on the tops. Keeps poachers off his land. Officiates when his lordship wants a shoot. That sort of thing. Soon his employer and his friends will be out shooting the grouse on the twelfth of August and Jim Edwards will be in charge of that.

'My nearest neighbour, old Jonas Bottomley, makes a few pounds for himself when that takes place by working as a beater. The rest of the time he spends making moonshine.'

'And I thought that the countryside was a quiet, law-abiding place,' Luke said in mock horror. 'What next?'

'Next are the house calls, I'm afraid. Are you ready?'

'Sure am,' he said easily, with no intention of telling her that he'd just had a phone call from the headmistress at Oliver's school to ask if he would make sure his nephew understood that he couldn't use his mobile phone in class.

'We are trying to be as lenient as possible with those two boys under the circumstances,' she'd said. 'But Oliver does take advantage of it sometimes. I am phoning you as he tells me that his mother has gone away and won't be back for some weeks.'

'Yes, phone me by all means if there is any problem at all with either Oliver or Owen,' he'd told her 'They *are* going through a difficult time, but I don't intend to let them misbehave if I can help it.'

When he got in that evening Rebekah Wainright was there, and to Luke's relief she turned out to be a much gentler soul than her friend Izzy Chambers. She was tall, slim and extremely neat, he noted. Probably in her late sixties and looking good for her years. She'd made a meal, cottage pie with an apple tart to follow, and he could have kissed her.

'I need to know what you are expecting of me, Dr Anderson,' she told him. 'Just make me a list, and I'll do my best to follow it. I didn't know whether you would want me to cook for you tonight, but I took the chance and will do so each time I'm here, but only if you want me to.'

'I most certainly do,' he told her. 'Where do you live, Mrs Wainright? I hope it isn't too far away for you. I'll be here to run you home in the evenings but I won't be around when you start in the middle of the day.'

'No problem,' she told him. 'I'm only just down the road. And before I go, what about those two lads? Is it all right to feed them when they get in from school? They were starving today so I gave them a glass of milk and some fruit to keep them going until you came home.'

'That is perfectly all right. Teenage boys have permanently empty stomachs when they're shooting up into adolescence.'

When she'd gone the three of them tucked into the food, and once their appetites were appeased Owen said, 'Can we go to Manchester on Saturday, Uncle Luke?'

'Er, yes, if you want,' he told him. 'What did you want to do there?'

'Bowling. And the cinema.'

'Fine, but you do realise I'll be going with you. I'm not letting you out on your own in the city. What about you, Oliver? Do you want to go?'

'Yeah,' Oliver said, his excited expression reminding Luke of the mothing excursion. 'But don't bring Dr Marshall this time, will you? It's boys only.'

'Sure, no problem,' Luke agreed, then said in a brisker tone, 'And now who has homework to do?'

There was silence.

'Come on, both of you, no slacking. If you don't do your homework we don't go bowling. And by the way, Oliver, as well as it being against the school rules, it is extremely rude to use your mobile in class. Don't do it.'

When they were settled, one at each side of the kitchen table, doing their homework, Luke went to ring Megan to report on Rebekah Wainright's first half-day at Woodcote House.

She might not be interested, he thought, but it would be a chance to hear her voice again, and to let her see that his domestic life was in control.

It had been good, their second day together in the practice. At least that was his opinion. But he'd started off on the wrong foot with Megan. It didn't follow that she'd felt the same.

* * *

Sighing, Megan flopped down on the sofa. She'd felt miserable when she and Luke had separated at the end of the day, and told herself it had to stop. If all *she* had in her life was the practice, it wasn't so for him. He had a grieving family to help get through some of the worst months of their lives, plus a business that he knew nothing about to oversee, *and* the position of village doctor to hold down.

She really couldn't see how she could fit into his scheme of things, even if he wanted her to, and the information, offered casually, that he'd long ago forgotten that she'd sent him a Valentine wasn't helping.

It was in the midst of those sombre thoughts that the phone rang and a voice said in her ear, 'I thought I'd let you know that Rebekah Wainright looks as if she's going to be a gem.'

'That's good,' she told him, suddenly feeling much happier, though she wished it was themselves that he'd rung to talk about. 'And the boys, are they all right without their mum?'

'They seem to be. They're doing their homework at the moment, reluctantly I might add. And what have you planned for the evening, Megan?'

'Chores,' she told him without much enthusiasm.

'Come round for supper, then.'

'I can't keep butting into their lives, Luke,' she said hesitantly.

'What about my life?' he questioned levelly 'I'm going to need some company to bring me back to adulthood occasionally. We're going bowling on Saturday and I've had instructions that I shouldn't ask you to join us. It's boys only.'

'That's fine with me,' she said with feeling. 'And in any case, I've already got something arranged. In Manchester, too, as it happens.'

He was immediately curious. 'Anything interesting?'

'To me, yes. I'm going to have a leisurely afternoon going around the shops and then I'm meeting one of my friends from university for a night at the ballet.'

'Sounds good. Is she anyone I might remember?'

'It's a he.'

'Oh, I see,' he said flatly, and wished he hadn't been so nosy. It served him right for not thinking there might be someone already in her life. Red-gold hair, green eyes and a fluid mover like Megan were not going to go unnoticed by his own sex.

'Am I likely to remember *him*, then?'

He was glad this conversation was taking place over the phone. If Megan could see his expression she would pick up on his dismay.

'Andy Warhurst.'

'Really! Then I'm presuming that he must have changed a lot,' he commented dryly. 'I remember him as disruptive whenever he chose to attend my lectures.'

At the other end of the line it was dawning on Megan that he was jumping to the wrong conclusions. She wouldn't be interested in Andy Warhurst in a thousand years, but maybe it would do no harm to let Luke think she might be.

The truth of it was that after they'd all left university, Megan had introduced Andy to Jenny, one of her childhood friends from the days when they'd been in the same ballet class. They'd fallen in love and got married, and now Jenny was a member of the company who were at present performing at a theatre in central Manchester.

Jenny had been the one most keen to make a career in ballet and she'd rung to ask Megan if she'd like to see the show. 'I'm only one of the chorus,' Jenny had said. 'But I've got two tickets. Andy is going to use one of them and I wondered if you would like the other.'

'Oh, yes!' Megan had said immediately.

'So would you feel like joining up with him?' Jenny had asked. 'It isn't really his scene, and I know he'd like to see you again. I promise that he's much better behaved these days,' she'd told her laughingly.

The arrangements had been made, and now Luke was getting his wires crossed.

'So how about supper, then?' Luke asked, returning to his earlier suggestion.

'I suppose I could pop down for half an hour.'

'Great, so we'll see you then.'

* * *

Her mother had phoned earlier and Luke had been the main topic of conversation.

'How are you and he getting along?' she'd wanted to know.

'Not bad so far. But it's early days yet.' Megan had told her. 'Luke is going to have his hands full on the domestic front for the next few weeks.'

'Why is that?'

'Sue has gone to France to stay with friends.'

'And taken the boys with her, I hope.'

'I'm afraid not. They didn't want to go, and in any case she couldn't take them out of school during term time.'

'So her brother has been left in charge of them?'

'Yes.'

'And the garden center, too?'

'Hmm. But I don't think that will give him much trouble. Everyone who works there is very loyal, and before you ask about the practice, Luke is spot on and determined not to let his other commitments interfere.'

'Good,' her mother said, and Megan knew she was saying what Margaret wanted to hear.

'Now, tell me about yourselves,' Megan coaxed, moving onto safer ground 'Are the house and its surroundings as wonderful as you remember them?'

'Absolutely. We're going to love it here, but only if you are happy back there in the village.'

'I'm fine,' Megan said, omitting to mention that she'd had grave doubts about the suitability of the man they'd found for her to share the practice with, and that they hadn't entirely disappeared.

And now she'd accepted his invitation to go for supper because she couldn't see enough of him. She was heading for a fall and knew it.

As she drove to Woodcote House in the summer dusk the village was quiet except for where the lights of The Badger spilled out across the main street. There was activity inside and outside of the old stone pub. There were those who'd taken their drinks outside into the balmy evening, and the rest who felt that the old settles inside were too comfortable to be exchanged for a hard wooden seat.

When she turned into the drive of Woodcote House, Luke was cutting the grass at the front, and down the side of the house she could see Owen and Oliver playing basketball.

To the onlooker it was a peaceful, domestic sort of scene, but she knew that there were undercurrents not visible to the uninformed. A missing mother trying to cope with an aching loss. Two young boys left fatherless, and in the middle of it a man that she'd once been attracted to and could be again. But she was on the edge of his life, coping with her own responsibilities, and if Luke let her down they would be twofold.

When he saw the car he switched off the mower and came across, smiling his welcome, and the boys came round from the back to see who was calling.

'Are we going mothing again?' Oliver asked eagerly when he saw her, and Luke shook his head.

'Just because Megan has arrived it doesn't

mean that another foray into the fields is on the cards. She's come to have supper with us. So I suggest that we all go inside and we three get washed up.'

'What are we having?' Owen asked, more interested in the menu than the niceties.

'Crumpets, cake and coffee,' Luke told him as the two doctors followed them into the house.

'Have you heard from Sue yet?' Megan asked.

'Yes. She rang a few moments ago to say she's arrived safely. Her friends were there to meet her at the airport, and once I'd assured her that all was well here, she sounded quite cheerful.'

'I was wrong to think it would be chaos, wasn't I?' Megan said wryly. 'Putting the gloom on everything before I'd seen you in action.'

'It's early days yet. Don't forget that when you were thinking those sort of thoughts, Sue hadn't found Rebekah for us, or Connie to keep the place clean, *and* I've still got to talk to Ned, who's the top guy in the garden centre. Even if he sees to the running of it, there will still be wages to be calculated and paid, materials to order and invoices to be dealt with. I'm going to pop back here in the lunch-hour tomorrow to have a quick word with him. We need to arrange a proper meeting. I can't let the business go to pot. Sue is going to need the money.'

Megan nodded. 'Did Gareth have life insurance?'

'Mmm, though it's not a fortune, I'm afraid. But you haven't come here tonight to be bogged down with this family's problems. Sue and the boys are my responsibility.'

'Not entirely, Luke. I've known her a long time and will help in any way I can.'

'Yes, I know you will, but you're not here for that now. Make yourself comfortable and I'll put the kettle on.'

Instead of doing as he'd suggested, Megan followed him into the kitchen. 'I'll do the crumpets if you like,' she volunteered, 'while you make the coffee.'

'Yes, all right,' he said. 'The boys have gone upstairs to spend a last hour on their own pursuits before going to bed. They'll come down for theirs when it's ready.'

'How are you going to make sure that Oliver doesn't try to slip out again when he thinks you're asleep?' said Megan, putting crumpets into the toaster.

'Simple. I make sure that he's asleep before I am.'

'And Owen. Is he likely to do that sort of thing?'

'Only time will tell.'

'You're very philosophical about all that has been thrust upon you.'

'What else can I be?'

It wasn't the moment to tell her that meeting her again was balancing the scales. That he'd been amazed when she'd appeared in his life again and was helping him to forget for a while the nasty taste that his divorce from Alexis had left.

Marriage to Alexis had been a short, sharp shock. They'd met at a party given by one of his medical associates and been immediately attracted to one another. She was tall, with striking good looks and a high opinion of herself as one of the top surgeons in the area.

A whirlwind romance had been followed by a smart wedding and no one had thought to tell him that he was just one in a long line of conquests. That he might have progressed further than the rest by being allowed to place a wedding ring on her finger, but it was unlikely to last.

His affection had been sincere and enduring, until he'd discovered that his new wife had found herself pregnant by him soon after they'd married and had had an abortion without his knowledge or consent.

She'd told him when it had been over and done with. In the row that had followed he'd wondered how he could have been so blind.

Her career came first, she'd said, and his anger had been directed at himself as well as Alexis. He'd taken it for granted that she would want a family as much as he did, and was about to pay for his mistake.

He had just fought his way through months of hell on earth when he'd received some

Valentines from the students he'd been lecturing and Megan's had been amongst them.

She'd already caught his attention before that because she had been so different from the woman he'd married. Small, serious, hardworking, and with hair and eye colouring so different from that of his sultry ex-wife he'd been reminded continually of his stupidity in rushing into a marriage with no foundations.

But he'd not been about to let his personal troubles affect his ethics and so had made no move to get to know Megan better. Now things were different, it seemed the fates had given him a push in her direction again.

This time there was going to be no rushing into the unknown, he'd decided. He would take it slowly and enjoy the pleasure of really getting to know her as a colleague and as a person.

When he'd decided to change his job, move house and come to help his bereaved sister and her children through some dark days, he hadn't bargained for it being quite so time-consuming, but that would pass, he told himself, and when it did Megan, of the red-gold hair and green eyes, would still be there.

He also hadn't bargained for a clash of temperaments almost as soon as he'd stepped over the threshold of the practice. But thankfully that storm was calming down. Tonight she was here beside him at Woodcote House and he wasn't complaining about that.

The crumpets were ready, and as she buttered them Megan said, 'I know you won't want me to be talking health care, but when you have some free time, if ever, I'd like us to discuss some improvements that I have in mind for the surgery.'

'Sure,' he said easily, ignoring the dig about his lack of free time. 'Concerning what? Fabric or function?'

'Both, but not tonight.'

He could agree on that, Luke thought. The boys had taken their supper upstairs and they were alone for a short time and the last thing he wanted to do was talk shop.

'So tell me about yourself, Megan,' he said when they were seated on opposite sides in the sitting room.

'What do you want to know?'

'What makes you tick.'

You do, she was tempted to say, but was pretty sure that wasn't what he meant.

'My job. I love it. Maybe because I've always been on the fringe of health care with both my parents being doctors. There was a time when I would have liked to make ballet my career, but medicine had a stronger pull.

'My friend, Jenny, who I'm going to see perform on Saturday night, was in the same ballet class as I was here in the village, but she's taken it further and now it's her full-time occupation.'

He nodded. 'I'd imagined that you'd had some sort of dance training from the way you move.'

'The way I move?'

'Mmm. There's a sort of fluid grace about your movements.'

'I suppose that ballet *does* do that for a person. Although I wasn't aware of it in my case,' she said as her heartbeat quickened. It was a compliment of sorts and she would treasure it. 'Is there anything else you want to know?'

'Are you in any kind of a serious relationship?' The question was a bit presumptuous and he thought it would serve him right if she told him to mind his own business. He watched her colour rise but the expected snub didn't come.

'No. Why do you ask?' Her tone was cool but not offended.

'Just that if you are, we might at some future date have to consider our positions.'

It was a weak excuse he was using for asking her, but it had put his mind at rest on one thing. He wasn't going to have to watch her with someone else. Yet what about Andy Warhurst, who was taking her to the ballet? God forbid! But he couldn't bring that up again. It would seem as if he doubted her word.

'And what about you?' she retaliated. 'The same applies if you should want to settle down with someone, and I do think that these sorts of questions are a bit premature, it being only our second day of working together.'

He ignored the last part of the sentence and said flatly, 'I've already been there and it was the worst thing I've ever done in my life. I showed complete lack of judgement and suppose I deserved all I got.'

'Do you want to tell me about it?'

'Not particularly, but I feel that maybe I should. So that you know where I'm coming from. Have you heard of Alexis Duncan, a surgeon who specialises in ear, nose and throat surgery?'

'Er, yes, of course. Who hasn't?'

'I was married to her for just a year before I filed for divorce.'

'I see.'

'I don't think you do,' he said sombrely, 'but I'd rather not discuss it further if you don't mind. Except to say that one can experience hell on earth if one is unfortunate enough.'

She could feel his hurt like a tangible thing, and there was raw pain mixed in with it that she would have expected to have lessened by now.

It was true that Alexis Duncan was someone she'd heard of but she'd never met her. Clever, very attractive and going places was how someone had once described her, and she wondered what it was that had made Luke file for divorce.

From what she'd seen of him since they'd met up again, he was no dunce himself. They must have been a striking couple on the outside, but something on the inside couldn't have been right.

Oliver and Owen appeared to say goodnight at that moment, so it brought an end to the strange conversation they'd been having, and as she looked at the man, and the boys who were going to be relying on him so much in weeks to come, Megan felt tears prick. Had anyone been there for Luke in the dark days of his divorce? she wondered. Probably not. But she'd only heard his side of the story.

When it was time to go he came out into the drive with her and as they stood uncertainly in the velvet darkness he said, 'We must do this again. Yes?'

'Yes. Why not?' she replied, but her voice lacked conviction and he thought he knew why. He'd brought the baggage of a failed marriage with him. It wasn't surprising if Megan wasn't impressed with that.

Her thoughts were running on similar lines as she drove home. Luke had mentioned his divorce before but only briefly, whereas tonight he had brought it out into the open, and she'd felt that the fact of it had tarnished the image she'd always had of him.

One thing she knew. She was going to find out more about Alexis Duncan, the woman he'd married. She had to see for herself what she was up against.

After those first few days of unease the rest of Luke's first week at the practice passed uneventfully, with staff and patients weighing up the new doctor and not finding him wanting.

If his home life was hectic he kept the fact to himself. He'd had a long conversation with Ned, who was in charge of the garden center, and had discovered that he knew every plant in the book, was reliable and trustworthy, but had no flair for figures. So he, Luke, was going to be burning some midnight oil regarding the garden centre until Sue came home.

He was half regretting agreeing to go to Manchester with the boys on the coming Saturday. Ned had impressed on him that Saturdays and Sundays were the busiest days in the garden centre and he felt that he should be out there giving a hand and keeping his eye on things.

But a promise was a promise and there was no way he was going to disappoint Owen and Oliver. They needed to feel they could rely on him and so far there had been no hitches.

On Friday afternoon Elise Edwards turned up at the antenatal clinic that Megan and one of the practice nurses ran each week, and as the young doctor flashed her a smile she rolled her eyes heavenwards and said, 'I still can't believe it, becoming parents again. Jim is over the moon, but the girls aren't exactly jumping for joy.'

'They will be when the baby arrives,' Megan said consolingly. 'They won't be able to resist him or her.'

'I hope you're right,' Elise said with a sigh. 'Sophie had the cheek to say, "Just supposing one of us was pregnant at the same time. How embarrassing can it get?"'

'What did you say to that?'

'That at sixteen she had better not be, and she was quick to assure me that she wasn't.'

'How far on do you think you are?' Megan asked.

'Two months. I'd just missed my second period when I came the other day.'

'Any nausea or tender breasts?'

'No sickness, but I have got some tenderness and I feel tired all the time.'

'That will be your body gearing itself up for the big job ahead of it during the coming months. It will adjust once the pregnancy really gets under way, and in the meantime don't overdo it. Eat lots of good food and get plenty of rest. What about the bakery? You're on your feet a lot.'

'We're trying to decide what to do about it. Whether I should get some extra help or sell up, but I love that shop. Just supposing I sold it and then lost the baby for some reason, and there is always the risk of Down's syndrome at my age, isn't there?'

Megan nodded. 'There is that risk, so you'll

need to decide if you would like to have an amniocentesis. It's not a risk-free procedure itself, however, and I'll give you all the information you'll need. Of course you are welcome to ask me any questions.' She went to her filing cabinet and pulled out some leaflets. 'The test is usually done from fifteen weeks. What happens is a needle is used to take a small amount of fluid from the amniotic sac, avoiding the foetus and placenta, and the fluid is sent for analysis. The test results are available one to three weeks later, and in the event that any chromosomal abnormalities are detected, you would need to consider whether you wished to continue with the pregnancy or not.'

The mother-to-be sighed. 'The more I think about it, the more I want this baby, but nothing in life is ever simple, is it? If I could give Jim a son he would be in heaven.'

'So let's wait and see, Elise,' Megan said gently. 'And in the meantime, if you go to the nurse she will check your blood pressure and will want a urine sample from you.'

As she got to her feet Elise said, 'You'll be around for me, won't you, Megan? You aren't thinking of doing the same as your parents and leaving Dr. Anderson in charge, are you? He's great, but we do need a woman in the practice.'

'No, of course I'm not thinking of leaving and following my parents!' she exclaimed laughingly. 'Luke and I are going to run the practice between us. Remember, I gave up my hospital job to come here. I've always loved this place. Nothing would induce me to leave the village now.' And as the other woman went to find the nurse Megan thought that the best reason in the world for not wanting to move was just a few feet away in the room next to hers.

CHAPTER FOUR

'HAVE a nice time at the ballet,' Luke said as the two doctors prepared to go their separate ways at the end of Friday's last surgery. 'If I had a choice that's where I would want to be going tomorrow.'

'The ballet? Really?'

'Yes. It's pure artistry. Music and movement at its best.'

'If that's how you feel, I'm sure that Andy won't mind you coming along,' she said laughingly.

'No, thanks. I am committed to a day of bowling and kids' films with my two young charges. You know very well I wouldn't break my word. When I make a promise, I keep it.'

'Wedding vows?' she questioned, and as soon as the words were out she wanted to take them back. It was an extremely intrusive thing to have said and brought coolness into the atmosphere.

'Don't judge me on matters that you know nothing of, Megan,' he said coldly, and got into his car and drove off.

As she watched him go Megan knew she'd made the comment out of pique. She didn't want Luke to have been married and divorced. *She* wanted to be the first woman in his life, but no matter what happened that was never going to be.

There was no longer a Saturday morning surgery at the practice, Until recently one of the doctors had been there from half past eight until ten o'clock for emergencies and the collecting of prescriptions. But the primary care trust had decided that they were no longer able to fund the arrangement and the Saturday morning surgery had been withdrawn, leaving Megan plenty of time to get ready for her day in Manchester instead of rushing home from the practice.

She'd been looking forward to it until she'd

said the wrong thing to Luke the night before and now the weekend lay ahead like an ordeal to be faced. They wouldn't meet again until Monday morning, unless she went round to Sue's place to try to make peace with him before travelling to Manchester.

But if the chill in his voice had been anything to go by, she would be the last person he wanted to see, she thought glumly, and for all she knew he and the boys might have already set off. So maybe leaving it until Monday might be the best idea.

In spite of her waning enthusiasm Megan dressed carefully for the day ahead in a long, black, tiered skirt and a cream jacket, and, with the thought of the theatre in the evening, piled her hair on top and secured it with a gold comb.

'Pity the man of your dreams isn't going to see you today,' she said to the reflection in the mirror, and set off for what the day might hold.

When she arrived at the small country station her eyes widened. They were there on the opposite platform. Luke and the boys. Owen and Oliver in jeans and brightly coloured

T-shirts and Luke similarly dressed but in a more subdued top.

As she moved towards him Megan's heartbeat was quickening. She wasn't going to have to wait until Monday. Luke was there, only yards away. But what sort of a reception was she going to get?

That question was not to be answered immediately. Oliver was observing her with wide blue eyes and saying, 'Uncle Luke, Dr Marshall can't come bowling dressed like that. They'll laugh at us. You said you would ask her not to come.'

'She isn't coming, Oliver,' he said, keeping a straight face. 'Dr Marshall is going to the ballet. It is just chance that we're on the same train.' He wasn't going to mention that they'd already let two trains go through on the off chance of meeting up with her.

His nephews hadn't commented as he'd managed to keep them entertained, so hopefully they wouldn't mention it either.

The Manchester train came at that moment and once they were seated Megan waited for a sign to tell her just how much she was out of favour. It didn't come as such. The first thing he said to her directly was, 'It would seem that you think Andy Warhurst is worth dressing up for.'

'Were you expecting me to go to the ballet in jeans?' she said. 'I know that lots of people do, but I'm not lots of people.'

'No, you are not, are you? You are someone who felt she had the authority to question my behaviour.'

He watched the colour rise in her face and knew he couldn't be angry with her for long. If Megan knew the full story of his ghastly marriage she would understand, but he wasn't touting for sympathy. And if he was, he didn't think he could bear to spell out the details.

'I am so sorry about that,' she said contritely. 'I was totally out of order. I don't know what got into me.'

She did, but wasn't going to tell him that she was jealous of the woman who'd found him first.

He smiled. 'Apology accepted. You don't beat about the bush when you've something to say, do you? I can be a bit like that myself, too.'

He was still smiling and she began to relax now that they were on speaking terms again. Maybe it was the moment to put him straight about herself and Andy, she thought, and clear the air all round.

'I'm not dressed up for Andy Warhurst,' she told him. 'We are merely keeping each other company during the performance. He's Jenny's husband. She said that ballet isn't really his kind of thing and asked me to join up with him until it was over.'

His expression had brightened. 'I see. Well, in that case give him my best regards and tell him I remember him well, but don't go into details.'

The train was pulling into Manchester's Piccadilly Station. It was time to separate and Luke wondered if she was as loth to part as he was, but the boys were tugging at him and he gave a wry smile.

'Duty calls, Megan. Have a lovely day. I'll see you on Monday.' And with that he was gone, following the boys out of the busy station.

* * *

'So what are you up to these days, Megan?' Andy asked in the interval at the ballet.

'I'm a country GP,' she told him, 'in the practice that used to belong to my parents before they retired.'

'And is that what you want for yourself?'

'Yes. I love it. What about you?'

'Registrar at one of the hospitals here in Manchester. The Ear, Nose and Throat.'

Megan's eyes widened in surprise. 'Is that the one where Alexis Duncan is a big noise?'

'Yes. Why?'

'Does the name Luke Anderson ring a bell?'

He frowned. 'Of course. Our tutor and ex-husband of the said Alexis.'

'He's my new partner in the practice.'

'What? Luke Anderson hibernating in the countryside.'

Megan smiled. 'He sends you his regards.'

'I'll bet,' Andy scoffed. 'There was nobody more surprised than him when I got my degree. Why has he moved onto your patch?'

'His brother-in-law died suddenly from a

heart attack. Luke has moved to the village to give some support to his sister and two sons.'

'He's a decent guy,' Andy admitted. 'His divorce from her majesty rocked the corridors of health care at the ENT. No one knew what she'd been up to, but he stood no messing. Alexis is so used to ruling the roost she was flabbergasted at the way she got her marching orders.

'Anderson was lecturing at that time and I thought he still was, but obviously not. How do you get on with him? I remember some of the girls at uni fancied him.'

'Yes. I was one of them,' she said laughingly. 'But I'm not sure that divorced men are in my line. We've only been working together for a week, so it's early days to be making a judgement.'

When the performance was over Jenny suggested that the three of them go for supper and Megan agreed, but warned her that the last train went at eleven-thirty and she didn't want to miss it.

'My car is parked at the other end,' she told

her, 'and then I've got to drive up the hill, so I definitely don't want to miss that train.'

She caught it with just minutes to spare and then sat back and let her mind go over the day's events. The ballet had been superb. It had been great to see Jenny and Andy but, ridiculous as it might seem, the highlight of the day had been the time she'd spent with Luke on the journey into Manchester.

The fact that Andy worked at the same hospital as Alexis Duncan had been a surprise, and no doubt he would have told her more about Luke's divorce if she'd egged him on. But she hadn't wanted that. If she ever found out the truth of it, she would want the words to come from the mouth of the man who'd come back into her life.

Just as Megan could see Woodcote House down below from the windows of her cottage, so, looking upwards, Luke could see her small residence high on the hill, and when it got midnight and the lights were still not on, he picked up the phone, thinking that maybe Megan had gone straight in and to bed.

He knew she wouldn't thank him if that was the case and his call brought her out of sleep, but was going to chance it. There was no answer and he knew she wasn't back.

At half past twelve he went to pick up the phone again, but at that moment the lights in the cottage came on and he breathed a sigh of relief. You are crazy, he told himself as he went up the stairs. As if you haven't taken on enough responsibility in this place, now you're fussing over someone who is perfectly capable of looking after herself. How do you think she coped before you appeared on the scene?

He didn't know. What he *did* know was that she was young, hard-working and beautiful, with her striking colouring and grace of movement, yet there didn't seem to be any potential boyfriends hovering. It would be so easy to fall in love again, but he'd rushed down that path once and it had been full of thorns.

After checking that the boys were where they should be at that hour, he went to bed himself, aware that it was Sunday already. Soon it would be Monday and with Monday came

Megan with the no-nonsense approach when it came to the practice, its patients *and himself.* With that thought he turned on his side and slept.

'How was your trip to the city?' Megan asked on Monday morning.

Luke smiled. 'Fine. We had a good day. I really enjoyed myself. Those are two great kids. And what about you? Did you enjoy the ballet?'

'Yes, I did. We went for a meal afterwards and I caught the last train with only minutes to spare.'

'I gathered that.'

'What do you mean?'

'I saw your lights go on at somewhere around midnight.'

'Oh, I see. Checking up on me, were you?'

'No, not really,' he said smoothly. 'I was admiring the night sky from my bedroom window and happened to see your place suddenly come to life.'

It wasn't true, of course. He had been checking on her, but only in the best possible way, and the thought came again that she'd managed to get along very well without anyone looking out for her welfare so far. If Megan knew what was in his mind, she would think he was crazy or some sort of opportunist.

'How did you get on with Warhurst?' he asked with a swift change of topic.

'All right. He was amazed to hear you were working as a GP here in the village. He's a registrar at the Ear, Nose and Throat,' she told him, and waited to see if he had any comment to make.

'Hmm, really. Good for him,' he murmured, settling himself behind his desk for the day ahead, and that was all. The last thing he wanted was for Alexis to crop up again. *She* was in the past, and as Megan left him without further comment, he thought that was where his ex-wife was going to stay.

A knock on the door as he was about to call in his first patient turned out to be Connie, the cleaner, asking if she could have a quick word.

'Yes, of course,' he said with a smile for the second of his two domestic lifelines. 'What can I do for you?'

Connie came to Woodcote House each day after she'd finished at the surgery in the early morning and they hadn't seen much of each other so far, but he had felt her presence when he'd gone home to find the place clean and tidy.

'I just wanted to ask if you are satisfied with what I'm doing, Dr Anderson,' she said nervously.

'Yes, of course I am,' he told her. 'I hope we don't leave you too much of a mess to clear up. Teenage boys are not the tidiest of creatures.'

She smiled. 'I know. I've had some myself.' Her nervousness came back. 'There is something else I wanted to ask you about. Could I have an appointment to see you?'

'Certainly. I'll see you now before you set off for my place, if you like, and before the surgery gets under way.'

Connie, who was in her late fifties, and trim with it, had the feet of someone who was on them too much. They were misshapen, with a bunion on each foot pushing the big toes sideways.

'Dr Marshall, Megan's father, was always on

at me to have the bunions removed, but I know what it would mean,' she said. 'Time off my feet, and when I did walk, plenty of pain.'

Luke nodded sympathetically. 'And you don't want to have to put up with that.'

'Not if I can help it. I've got a sick husband.'

'Do you have children who could help out?'

She shook her head. 'They're all married and living away. What I came for really was to ask what *you* thought I should do.'

'I think you should have the bunions removed,' he told her. 'You're still a comparatively young woman. Your feet will only get worse. Why not let me make an appointment for you to see someone about them? At least then you'll know what would be involved and can take it from there.'

'What about my cleaning for you? I would be letting you down if I decided to be operated on.'

Luke frowned. 'Nothing of the kind. It could be a while before they operated, and if you don't get it sorted it's yourself that you'll be letting down. So tell me, do I write to the hospital or not, Connie?'

'Yes, all right, then, if you will, Doctor,' she said reluctantly.

'You're not committing yourself to anything by seeing an orthopaedic consultant,' he reminded her as she got ready to leave, 'but if you don't get some professional advice you'll never know what is involved.'

After surgery, Megan popped in to see him. 'I saw Connie come in this morning. What did she want?'

'She wanted to see me about her feet. I was surprised that she didn't ask you for advice.'

Megan sighed. 'She's already done that and knows what I think. We've discussed it often enough. I've told her to get them put right before they get any more deformed.'

'I see. So it wasn't my charm that made her come to me. She was possibly hoping that I would say something different.'

'And did you?'

'No. Of course not. Anyone can see that she needs surgery. What about her sick husband, though?'

'Yes. That would be a problem. Dennis has

Parkinson's disease and needs some degree of help. He would have to go into care for a while if she went into hospital. But we are presuming too much, I fear. Connie won't even go to see someone to find out what needs doing.'

'That is in the past,' he said whimsically. 'I've persuaded her to let me make an appointment with one of the orthopaedic guys.'

'Really? Well done! So it must have been your charm after all. Maybe we should start a system where you see all the ditherers and difficult ones, and I jog along with the uncomplicated cases.'

'On your bike!' he told her, and saw amusement in the glance meeting his.

'Well, you are the senior doctor, remember. Mum and Dad chose you because you have a lot more experience than I have and they didn't want to leave me floundering.'

It was his turn to be amused. 'Floundering! That is not a term I would use to describe you. *I* may have the experience, but *you* have the advantage.'

'In what way?'

'In that everyone who comes through the surgery door knows and trusts you. Whereas the other day I heard a patient ask another why someone like me is working in a country practice, and the person replied that maybe I'd been struck off and this was all I could get.'

'I could make a guess who they were,' she said, smiling at the thought of what he'd just described. 'Two elderly ladies in pale blue fleeces with knitted hats.'

'Yes! Spot on.'

'They are the Rigby sisters, who until recently always asked to see my mother. Now she's gone they've reluctantly transferred themselves to me. One of them has thyroid problems, and the other is just getting over an attack of polymyalgia. You'll have two big disadvantages in their opinion. First, that you're a man and, second, that you aren't local.'

'Ah! So it's because I'm not a member of the clan.'

'Yes, but not as far as I'm concerned. I welcome the change. We need some new blood in the practice and I feel that we are fortunate to have you.'

Luke smiled. 'You weren't of that opinion during my first week here, were you?'

'No, I wasn't. My parents had always run this place like clockwork and I was apprehensive at being left to cope with a stranger. When you appeared I couldn't believe my eyes. It was like a burden being lifted off my shoulders, until I knew what was going to be happening in your life, and then the anxiety came back.'

She wasn't going to tell him just how much it had meant, discovering that he was her parents' choice, because the incident of the Valentine card was still there to take the edge off her pleasure, and even more so the knowledge that Luke had been married before.

It wasn't surprising. He was far too fanciable to be overlooked by her own sex. That was how it had been at university amongst the students he'd taught. All of them aware of his attractions, but at that time none of them had known he was married to the star of Ear, Nose and Throat and that it was he who was ending the marriage.

* * *

When she'd been to buy something for her lunch from Elise's bakery, Megan went to sit beside the river that flowed behind the practice. In all the village it was her favourite spot, as familiar to her as her own face. She knew every twist and turn of it. Every stone on its rocky bed. All the wildlife there, from the rarely sighted moorhen to the green finches, kingfishers and the heron, lording it over all with its long neck and large wingspan.

When she looked up, Luke was walking towards her, eating a sandwich. He dropped down beside her on the grassy bank and asked, 'So what river is this?'

'The Goyt,' she told him. 'It joins the Etherow in the next village.'

He nodded thoughtfully. 'Whatever happens with Sue and the boys, I won't want to be leaving this place in a hurry. It's like another life, living here.' His gaze was on the skyline. 'Are you ever called out to visit patients up there?'

'Yes. Though not too often, as there are only a few scattered farms and the odd cottage up on the tops. But if a call comes we go, and it can be scary if there is snow or high winds across the moors. You'll need to keep a shovel in the boot of your car.'

'I can see the sense of that. Have you ever been in difficulty up there?'

'No, not really, but my dad once had a narrow escape when his car was stuck in a snowdrift for hours on end. It took the police and mountain rescue to bring him to safety.'

In contrast to what they were discussing, it was a golden day, but there was a nip in the air, and when she shivered Luke said, 'Maybe we should make tracks.'

Taking her hand in his, he helped her to her feet and when they were facing each other he looked down on to the hand that lay in his and said, 'No rings. No wedding band or engagement ring. I would have thought that the men around here would have been queueing up.'

'A lot of men are nervous of women doctors,' she said lightly. 'They think if they marry one she'll have them forever at the gym, on vitamin pills and eating lettuce all the time instead of steak.'

'Rubbish!' he said laughingly. 'I would expect your unmarried state to be more because you are hard to please.'

'It might be,' she conceded. 'Whatever the reason, I'll know when the time is right.'

'I would hope so,' he told her, and wasn't quite sure what he'd meant by that.

Amongst those waiting to see Megan that afternoon was Tom Meredith, who owned the general store that housed the post office. It was a busy, friendly, place where nothing was too much trouble for its owner and his staff, but today Tom looked tense and tight-jawed.

In his late fifties and happily married to Sara, who looked after the post office side of things, he had two sons in their thirties. Josh, the elder, was suffering from alcohol-related acute liver failure. He needed a transplant desperately.

All the time that he'd been ill Tom and Sara had put on a brave front before their customers and staff, but today Tom looked like a man in deep despair. and what he had to say fitted in with that.

'I wanted a word with you, Megan, before Sara and I approach the hospital,' he told her. 'Josh is going to die if a liver doesn't become available soon. We've been wondering if part of one of our livers could be transplanted into him? We've heard of it being done successfully and we can't stand by watching him like this any longer. What do you think the chances would be?'

Her expression was grave. 'Under normal circumstances I would say it might be possible, Tom. But your circumstances are different, aren't they? Josh is adopted. So in the matching-up process you and Sara would be no different than any other member of the public.

'By all means put it to those who are treating Josh, but I doubt if they'll agree. If they operated and it wasn't successful, he mightn't be strong enough for further surgery when a liver comes through the usual channels.'

He nodded sombrely. 'Yes. I know what you mean, but I'm going to ask them. We just can't face up to losing him. We love those lads as if they are our own, and now Josh is facing up to all the drinking he did when he was in his teens. The poor boy was so messed up when he came to us. He's come a long way since then, and now this has happened.'

He got up to go. 'Thanks for your time, Megan,' he said quietly. 'Only a miracle will save him and there aren't many of those about these days.'

When she told Luke about Tom and Sara's dilemma he said, 'They'll have to hope that a liver comes available soon. I can't see any other way. There might have been a slight chance if they'd been the lad's natural parents, but as they're not…'

She nodded. 'In times of desperate need we clutch at straws, don't we? I've never yet been in that sort of situation, but I can imagine what it's like, and time is running out for Josh.'

'It can't always be easy for you, treating people who are friends and acquaintances,' Luke commented.

'It isn't. But there is often relief on the part of the patient to be dealing with someone who isn't a stranger. Though it does make me inclined to take their problems home with me.'

'That I can believe,' he told her. 'Yet you know, Megan, I've lived with someone high on the ladder of health care, in *her* opinion and everyone else's. It's good to work with someone who really cares about her patients.'

Megan could feel her colour rising. She supposed it was something if Luke approved of her as a doctor. How he saw her as a woman was another matter. He may have been unhappy with Alexis Duncan, but she would be some act to follow when it came to style and allure.

Luke's glance was on her face. It had attracted him long ago in the days when she'd been a serious student and he'd been full of rage and bitterness at the loss of his child. A child that he hadn't even known existed until Alexis had decided to put him in the picture.

But now his attention had shifted. He was looking past her and said, 'Hello, hello! Here comes trouble.' When she turned Megan saw Owen standing just inside the doorway of the surgery.

'I've lost my mobile, Uncle Luke,' he said miserably. 'Either that or someone's taken it.'

'Yes, but what are you doing here?' Luke asked. 'School isn't over for another hour and a half.'

'I slipped out at breaktime because I'm desperate to find it. I need my mobile.'

'No, you don't. Now get back to school fast before you're missed.'

'I can't go back there without it!'

'Oh, yes, you can. We'll sort out the phone business this evening. So on your way, Owen.'

'I've got a spare phone,' Megan said quickly, touched by the boy's distress. 'I've never used it, so it hasn't got anything private in it. You can borrow it until yours turns up if you like.'

Owen's expression indicated that the sun had just come out from behind a cloud. 'Yes, please, Dr Marshall. I'll take great care of it.'

'You'd better,' Luke told him.

'I'll get it. It's in my desk drawer,' she told

him, and within minutes Owen had gone with a lighter step than when he'd come in.

'You didn't have to do that, Megan,' Luke said when he'd gone. 'It would have taught him to be more careful with his things if he'd had to do without.'

'He's already doing without,' she reminded him. 'He's without a father and his mother is far away. I said I would do all I could to help, and compared to what you're doing for the boys it was a drop in the ocean.'

He nodded. 'Yes. You're right. Finding the right level between love and discipline isn't easy.'

'You'll make a great father some day,' she said impulsively, and saw his face close up.

'Chance would have been a fine thing,' he commented levelly, and wondered what the child that Alexis had aborted would have been like. Maybe she'd done them a favour. For children to be born into an unhappy marriage was not a good thing. It was a fallacy that their arrival brought peace to a warring couple.

Megan turned away. She wasn't going to ask what he'd meant. The tone of his voice told her not to. So instead she smiled and said, 'There's no rush to get the phone back. We can't have Owen upset and fretting. And by the way, have you been mothing of late? Any more journeys into the dark country night?'

Back to his usual equable self, he said, 'A couple of times, as I did make young Oliver a promise, you know.'

'Yes. I know you did *and* I know that you keep your promises,' she told him, with the memory crystal clear of when she'd questioned his keeping of his marriage vows.

'And how do you know that when you've no proof of it?'

'I'm not sure, but I do.'

'Mmm. I see.' He was glancing at the clock, and as if what they'd been discussing was of no merit he said, 'Shall we see how many people are waiting to see us? Hopefully with problems less dreadful than Tom Meredith's.'

CHAPTER FIVE

SEPTEMBER had gone, taking with it mellow days and cooler nights, and now October had arrived with a mixture of weather that was giving frequent reminders that winter was on its way.

The practice was running well. Megan's concerns regarding Luke's responsibilities seemed to have been unfounded as he was coping brilliantly, with his elderly housekeeper and not so elderly cleaner there to assist. There were times when he looked frayed around the edges but it didn't affect his good humour.

Any further trips to the city had been put on hold because he was spending any spare time in the garden centre, helping out and supervising generally.

His two nephews seemed more settled as the

weeks went by, and now the only problem was their mother, who was showing no signs of coming back to face up to life in the village with a family to care for and a business to run.

When Megan asked Luke about it he said sombrely, 'I think that Sue is afraid of having to cope without Gareth when she comes back, and keeps putting it off.'

'And so what does she intend doing?' Megan asked levelly. 'Has she forgotten that there are two fatherless boys here who aren't seeing much of their mother either? She's not being fair to them…or you.'

'Sue can't stay away for ever, Megan.'

'Oh, no? She's my friend but I do feel she's taking advantage of you, Luke.'

'Shall I be the judge of that?' he said coolly, even though he knew she was right. He wanted to tell her that when Sue came home there would be time for them and not just at the practice.

It was the end of the day. They were on the point of leaving the surgery, and he little knew that his recent complacency regarding Owen and Oliver was about to receive a severe jolt.

As he and Megan were going to their cars one of the receptionists came hurrying after them. 'Phone call for you, Dr Anderson,' she cried. 'It's Rebekah Wainright. There's been an accident at Woodcote House. One of the boys has been hurt.'

Megan watched the colour drain from his face. 'What sort of an accident?' he cried.

'They lit a firework that someone had given them and…'

She was talking to his departing back as he flung himself into his car. He'd heard enough. So had Megan, already in the passenger seat, and within minutes they were pulling up in front of the house.

They found Rebekah round the back of the house, bending over Oliver, while Owen, as white as a sheet, stood sniffling nearby. When she saw them she cried, 'I've sent for an ambulance. The firework went off with an awful blast and he was too near. Didn't move away quickly enough and he's been unconscious ever since.'

As the two doctors dropped to their knees beside him Luke said, 'He's breathing, thank goodness. Fast and irregular pulse, and burns down the side of his face.'

'I'll put a dressing on them while you keep a check on his breathing,' Megan said, thankful that he'd had a first-aid kit in the car. She was trying to keep calm for Luke's sake. The boys doing this was the stuff that night-mares were made of.

'They'd asked me about fireworks and I gave them all the warnings,' he said raggedly. 'I had no idea they might get one themselves—which just goes to show how wrong I was.'

'We got it off a boy outside the fish and chip shop,' Owen told them tearfully. 'He said it was a bargain for five pounds.'

'Do you think it was a bargain now?' Luke asked grimly, pointing to where Oliver was beginning to come round. 'I can't believe you'd put your brother at risk, Owen. Especially after I warned you. Thank good-ness Mrs Wainright was here.'

An ambulance arrived and as Oliver was being stretchered on board Owen began to cry. 'I want to go with him,' he sobbed. 'Is Oliver going to die, too?'

Luke's face was grey and pinched-looking as he comforted him and assured him that Oliver was going to be all right, but he needed to go to hospital to be treated for the burns and any other injuries that he might have sustained.

'Tell us what happened, Owen,' he asked gently, as he sat beside him in the ambulance.

'There was a big flash and it knocked him over,' he gulped.

Megan was seated facing them and as Luke shook his head in disbelief their glances met. Don't let him blame himself for this, she was thinking. Oliver is alive, thank goodness, and once we get him to A and E they'll sort him out.

'Don't tell Mum what we did, will you?' Owen pleaded as the ambulance sped towards the city.

'I'll have to,' Luke told him. 'I can't keep something like this from her, but don't worry. Once she knows you're both all right I'm sure she'll understand that you won't ever do it again. They'll most likely keep Oliver in hospital for a few days, so she'll have to know.'

Oliver was seen by a doctor in A and E and his burns were treated. They were mainly surface injuries on the side of his face and one of his forearms as he'd tried to shield himself from the exploding firework.

They'd been warned that there might be concussion from the way he'd been thrown by the blast and, as Luke had expected, they were going to be keeping him in for a few days for observation.

Luke and Megan were concerned that Oliver's hearing seemed to be affected, and now that he was fully conscious he was saying that it hurt when he swallowed.

There'd been no visible signs of injury to his throat, but the doctor in A and E recommended that he see an ear, nose and throat consultant to be on the safe side, and to Luke's dismay he said he would ask Alexis Duncan to have a look at him.

Megan saw Luke's expression, but knew he wouldn't think of objecting if the doctor in A and E was going to get the best for Oliver. His own feelings he would put to one side for his nephew, and as for herself, she hadn't yet made any effort to put herself in a position where she would be able to form an opinion about Luke's ex-wife, but now that the opportunity was being offered, she knew that it was what she wanted.

'Alexis is a friend of mine,' the A and E doctor told them. 'She's picking me up when I've finished here and we're going for a meal. So I'm going to ask a favour of her.'

It was nine o'clock when the woman who'd broken Luke's heart came to Oliver's bedside. When she saw him sitting there with Megan by his side, her dark almond-shaped eyes widened and she breathed, 'Luke! What are *you* doing here?'

'The boys are my nephews,' he said evenly. 'They've been playing with fireworks.'

'I see. So how are you?'

'I'm fine, Alexis,' he told her, 'and thanks for

coming to see Oliver. His father died recently and his mother is out of the country, so life hasn't been treating him very well of late, and now this.'

Her glance had switched to Megan, who was taking in every detail of the woman who had been Luke's first love.

'So you're not their mother, then.'

Before she could reply he said, 'Megan and I are jointly in charge of a country practice, and she is a friend of the boy's mother. It's been a long day for all of us. So if you wouldn't mind…'

Alexis was dressed for going out, in a long black evening dress relieved with expensive jewellery, but she nodded and bent over Oliver, who was regarding her dubiously.

'Can you hear what I'm saying, Oliver?' she asked.

'Not very well,' he said.

She'd brought her equipment with her, obviously having been warned about what lay ahead, and she looked into his ears for quite some time before asking him, 'Did the firework go off very close to you?'

He gazed at her blankly and she repeated the question in a louder voice and was told, 'Yes. It was a big bang.'

'I see. Will you open your mouth for me now while I look down your throat?'

Next she felt his neck glands and then looked into his ears once more, and when she'd finished she told them, 'I think the firework exploding so close has caused temporary deafness, which should gradually disappear, as fortunately there has been no piercing of the eardrums.

'His throat seems fine, and the fact that it hurts when he swallows will be muscular, probably from the same cause. That too should soon go away, but if it doesn't, you know where to find me, Luke,' she told him meaningfully, and then swept out of the ward to join her dinner date.

When the night sister on the children's ward took over she said, 'Why don't you go and get something to eat while I settle this young man for the night? He and his brother can have some supper up here.'

As they pointed themselves towards the hospital restaurant Luke said, 'Thanks, Megan.'

'What for?'

'Being there for us.'

'What about Alexis?' she asked. 'Giving her time and talents for *you*?'

'She was doing it to impress her latest conquest, not me,' he said dryly. 'She didn't know I was involved until she walked into the ward, and, believe me, she was the last person I wanted to see tonight, or at any other time for that matter.'

'What did she do to you that hurt so much?'

She couldn't have asked him under normal circumstances, but tonight everything seemed sharp-edged and important.

He sighed heavily. 'Alexis was pregnant and never told me. I was only informed when she'd had a termination.'

'Why?' Megan cried in horror. 'Why did she do that?'

'She said that her career came before a family. You can guess the rest.'

'That was unforgivable.'

'Yes, it was,' he agreed tonelessly as he guided her to an empty table in the restaurant. 'I hope that fellow in A and E knows what he's letting himself in for.'

She'd been ravenous before, but when Megan began to eat the food in front of her she found that she'd lost her appetite. It had been a horrendous few hours, and what Luke had told her was just as awful.

'Eat up,' he said gently. 'There's no cause for you to be upset. I don't want my affairs to put a blight on your life. The Alexis business is over, done with. And the next ghastly thing I've got to face is phoning Sue to tell her what's happened, and I am not relishing the thought of *that*.'

When they arrived back on the ward Oliver was asleep and Owen was watching television while he waited for their return. As Luke stood gazing down at his injured nephew, Megan thought how life could be so unfair. His own child was lost to him, but it didn't stop him from having this great affection for someone else's.

'So what's the plan?' she asked softly. 'Are you going to stay the night?'

'Yes.'

'What about Owen? Shall I take him home with me?'

He shook his head. 'No, Megan. You'll have

enough to cope with, facing up to my patients as well as your own in the morning. There is an overnight stay room just down the corridor. I'll check with Sister to see if I can bed Owen down in there for the night. Once it's been agreed I'm going to phone for a taxi for you, and during the quiet hours I'll phone Sue.'

He went to the main door with her when the call came that the taxi had arrived and held her close for a moment.

'I'm letting you down, Megan, aren't I?' he said in a low voice. 'Just as you knew I would.'

Green eyes flashed. 'Surely you don't think I am so mean-minded as to blame you for something like this!' she flared.

'You might feel differently in the morning when I'm missing from the practice.'

'Really! I'll be the judge of that. And if you think I can't manage the practice on my own, watch me!'

He didn't take her up on that, just said, 'Goodnight, Megan. Sweet dreams.'

* * *

Sweet dreams! she thought as the taxi took her homewards. Was he kidding? It would be surprising if she slept a wink after what he'd told her about his marriage break-up. Luke was meant to be a family man, not an embittered divorcee. She'd seen him with Owen and Oliver and he was incredibly loving and understanding.

She'd told him not long ago that he would make a wonderful father, having had no idea of what had gone wrong in his marriage. But the woman in the black dress had denied him that. Alexis had seen family life as a millstone, not a joy, and had done what suited *her* best.

She'd already been feeling fraught before that, because of the boys' foolish actions, and the possible consequences. But what Luke's ex-wife had done seemed deliberately cruel. There was an excuse for the boys' youthful stupidity, but not for what Alexis had done to Luke.

The taxi driver had driven past Woodcote House on the way home and she'd seen that Rebekah had locked up and everywhere was in darkness. She wanted to thank her for her prompt actions at the time of the firework explosion and asked him to stop briefly at her house as she could see a light on inside.

'How is Dr Anderson?' Rebekah asked after Megan had told her what was going on with Oliver.

'Devastated,' Megan told her. 'He's staying the night at the hospital and Owen is with him. When I left he was about to phone their mother to let her know what has happened. To receive that kind of news when one is far away must be dreadful.'

And now, at last, she was home. When she looked at her face in the bathroom mirror she groaned. Two eyes, black-ringed with fatigue, stared back at her, and the white shirt she'd worn for work was filthy from the smoke that had blackened everything near where the firework had gone off.

Her appearance was hardly what she would have chosen for being introduced to Alexis, but that was the least of her worries. Supposing

Oliver's hearing had been affected? she thought. Or his burns were more serious than they'd anticipated? And would this last catastrophe throw Sue into an even bigger black hole of despair and grief?

And there was Luke in the middle of it all. In charge of Owen and Oliver, the house and the garden centre. Doing everything right and yet it kept going wrong. When she'd sent him the Valentine card in her student days it had been his physical attractions alone that had been the reason for her youthful infatuation.

She'd had no knowledge of the integrity and stamina of the man underneath until now, and with each passing day her feelings for him were deepening.

Were they ever going to find time to really get to know each other? she wondered. It was one thing after another. He'd been quick to point out that he wouldn't be available for morning surgery tomorrow.

Her anxieties that he might let her down because of all his other commitments had come home to roost. Yet what could she do? She'd been angry at the way he'd taken it for granted that all she could think about was the practice. It wasn't Luke's fault that teenage boys behaved like teenage boys. Better that he'd been there to deal with what happened instead of their mother.

At eight o'clock the next morning she'd had breakfast and was about to leave for the surgery when there was a knock on the door. When she opened it Luke was standing there, looking more spruce than when she'd left him the night before.

As she stepped back to let him in he said, 'Owen and I have been to the house. We've both had a shower and some breakfast and I've just dropped him off at school. Now I'm on my way back to the hospital.'

'How is Oliver?' she asked anxiously.

'He's had a restless night, but was asleep when I left him.' He was observing her keenly. 'What about you, Megan? Are you all right?'

'Yes, I'm fine,' she told him, putting the night's worries to the back of her mind. 'Did you manage to get hold of Sue?'

'Yes. She's on her way home. She was fortunate to get an immediate flight.'

'And how was she?'

'Better than I expected. Awful though it is, she needed something like this to give her the impetus to come home. It's brought her back to reality.'

'That's good, but, as you say, what a shame it has to be for such an upsetting reason.'

She was checking the time. 'I'll have to be making a move, Luke.'

'Me, too,' he said. 'I can't linger. A doctor is coming to see Oliver at nine o'clock, and I'm told by Alexis's friend in A and E that she will be calling to see him again later in the morning.'

'How do you feel about that?'

'If she's keeping an eye on Oliver, fine. I won't allow the fact that she never did *me* any good to come into it.'

'Those boys come before anything else,' she said gently. 'Before you, before me, before Alexis, or anyone else for that matter. I am so thankful that Oliver escaped with as little hurt as he did.'

'So am I,' he said tersely, 'but there's still the matter of his hearing. We'll have to see how it is when he wakes up. The explosion blew out the windows in their bedrooms, with them being at the back of the house, so it's easy to see that it was some bang. They'll need replacing before it starts raining, and we might get burgled. Is there anyone among your village friends who could sort that out for me?'

'Yes,' she said promptly. 'You remember Josh Meredith, who's waiting for a liver transplant?'

'Not him, surely!'

'No. Of course not. But his elder brother, Jack, is a joiner. His place is at the end of Rabbit Lane. He's efficient and doesn't charge the earth. I've got his phone number somewhere. I'll ask him to give you a call. Now, hadn't you better go in case Oliver is awake and fretting?'

He nodded. 'Yes. I'll be able to tell him that his mum will be with him soon and that should cheer him up. I'll phone you at the surgery later to let you know what's going on. And, Megan, one of the reasons I've called is to apologise for being so tactless last night. Am I forgiven?'

'It's forgotten. I shouldn't have snapped at you.'

'It won't always be like this.'

'Would you like to bet on that?' she said dryly. 'What's that you have in your hand?'

He looked down on to the sheaf of papers he was carrying. 'They're the worksheets for the garden centre. The figures that I calculate the wages from. I thought I could do them while Oliver is waiting to see the doctors.'

'I rest my case,' she told him, and with no answer to that he went off into the October morning.

As Megan drove to the practice, Tom Meredith came hurrying out of the post office and waved her down. Tears were streaming down his face and she thought dismally, Please, don't let it be Josh.

As she rolled down the car window he sobbed, 'They've found him one, Megan! They've found a liver for Josh. They're going to do the transplant today. His mother and I are about to set off for the hospital now.'

She let out a sigh of relief. 'Oh! Tom! That's marvellous. I thought you were going to tell me the worst, and it's the *best*.'

'Aye. At least he's got a chance now. We'll just have to hope he's strong enough to cope with the surgery. The lad's very poorly.'

'We'll all be thinking of him, Tom, and wishing him well,' she said comfortingly.

'The foolishness of youth, eh, Megan?'

'Yes, indeed. One of Dr Anderson's nephews is in hospital after they set off a very powerful firework without permission.'

'Oh, dear! I'll tell Sara and we'll pop in to see him while we're there. It will be hours before there is any news for us.'

As Tom went hurrying back inside Megan thought how Luke envied her the friendships and acquaintances she had with the villagers. As well as sharing their good times, she suffered with them when things weren't so good, and she wouldn't change it for the world.

* * *

With two lots of patients to see, the morning flew with not a moment to spare and just as she'd said goodbye to the last of them and was about to set out on the house calls, her Aunt Izzy phoned.

'So what's this that Rebekah tells me about those boys from Woodcote House?' she asked immediately. 'Trying to blow the place up, were they?'

'Almost, Aunt Izzy,' Megan told her. 'Hopefully they've learned their lesson. Owen is all right, but Oliver has burns and some hearing loss at the moment, which we are hoping is only temporary.'

'Hmm. I see.'

'I'm going to have to go,' Megan said. 'I've my house calls to do and I'm late already.'

'I suppose *he's* at the hospital with them,' she said, ignoring Megan's comments about how busy she was.

'If you mean Dr Anderson, yes, he is, and now, if you don't mind, Aunt, dear—'

'It would seem as if Gareth Standish can rest easy with his brother-in-law on the scene,' her aunt went on, determined to say her piece, 'but he'll need eyes in the back of his head with those two. I've sent some bottles of my home-made elderflower cordial for them with Rebekah.'

Megan was laughing. 'You are something else,' she told her. 'Hard on the outside and soft as putty where your heart is.'

She heard the old lady chuckle at the other end of the line. 'It doesn't do to let folk see you're soft. Especially menfolk. Bear that in mind, my dear.'

A doctor had been to see Oliver on the children's ward and pronounced him to be recovering satisfactorily. Some of his hearing loss had gone and his throat muscles seemed to be less painful and in good working order. The day staff had put fresh dressings on the burns and now he was waiting eagerly for his mother to arrive.

When Alexis arrived he and Luke were just finishing a board game, with Oliver delighted to have won and Luke pretending disappointment.

She looked rather at a loss and Luke hid a smile. Alexis was used to having the full attention of those present when she entered a room, but not this time. He appreciated her making the effort to see Oliver again and would tell her so, but that would be it.

His mind was full of a young doctor with red-gold hair and green eyes, who moved with grace and purpose, loved her job, and was having to put up with a clever-clogs like him, who had a high opinion of his capabilities.

When Alexis had finished examining Oliver she said, 'The hearing is better this morning, don't you think?'

Yes, I do,' he agreed. 'It is a relief, and Sister said he ate his breakfast without any trouble, so it would appear that the throat strain has eased off.'

'When are they sending him home?'

'I don't know yet. His mother is due home from France any time and she'll be coming straight here.'

Alexis was getting ready to go and said, 'I don't think you need me any more, but give me a call if you do.'

He nodded. Alexis was the only person he knew who could put two double meanings into one sentence. She was asking if it really was all over and telling him to ring her if it wasn't.

'Thank you for your time,' he told her politely. Then he almost laughed when she said, 'Where shall I tell my secretary to send the account?'

'No need. I'll settle it now,' he told her, taking out his cheque book. There was no way he was going to give details of his whereabouts to her. But having got the message, she waved him away and sauntered out of the ward in search of someone she *could* manipulate.

By the time Megan got back from the house calls, a pale sun had come out. Taking advantage of it, she went down to her favourite place on the riverbank to eat her lunch.

It was too chilly to sit, so she leaned against the trunk of an old oak tree and munched away thoughtfully, until a shadow fell across her and Luke was there.

'I thought I might find you here,' he told her.

'I've come to do the afternoon surgery. Oliver is better this morning and he's with his mother. Sue arrived an hour ago and as they're not going to need me for a while, here I am. What's been happening while I've been absent?'

'Some good news. Josh Meredith is being given a liver transplant as we speak.'

'Really? That's great.'

'And Aunt Izzy has sent you some of her home-made elderflower cordial.'

'Nice! To what do we owe that honour?'

'It's her way of saying that she approves of you. Did Alexis put in an appearance?'

'Er, yes, briefly. I thanked her for her time and she asked me where she should send the account.' He was smiling, but it didn't reach his eyes. 'It would seem that nothing changes.'

'So what did you do?'

'Called her bluff. Got out my chequebook to settle it on the spot and she just waved it away and went. But I haven't come back to talk about Alexis. You're the one who's been on my mind all the time I've been at the hospital.'

'What about the wages for the garden center?' she teased. 'Don't tell me I came before them.'

'I managed to get them done, but my powers of concentration weren't at their best.'

'And what are they like now?'

'Fully keyed in. It's a pity that duty calls. I would love to explore the river with you.'

'We should have done it before the summer went,' she told him, and as two brightly painted canoes sailed past at that moment, with those who were paddling them shouting cheerful greetings, she went on, 'But it's never too late. Once things have settled down at Sue's place, I'll show you all my favourite haunts, but this is top of the list.' She smiled. 'If I ever get married I want it to be here on the riverbank where I make my vows.'

He raised his eyebrows. 'That could be a bit tricky.'

'Mmm. I know. But that is what I would want.'

'You said "if ever I get married", which makes it sound as if you have doubts regarding it. Have you?'

'I have one, yes.'

'What is it?'

They were on a delicate subject, she thought uneasily. Both were eager to know each other better, but if she spoke the truth it could bring an end to that. And if she didn't she might regret it later in their relationship.

She took a gamble and knew as the words came out of her mouth that it was a mistake. 'I would want to be the first love of the man I married.'

'I see,' he said flatly. 'It's understandable, I suppose. No one could blame you for that. I'm sure there must be lots of men who would be happy to have you as their first love.'

But not me, he thought as he left her to finish her lunch and went back to the surgery. *He* didn't have the right. He'd forfeited it because of one big mistake.

Megan was a great one for straight talk. He supposed he should be thankful for that, and put those sort of thoughts out of his mind, if it was possible.

CHAPTER SIX

As SHE watched Luke stride back into the surgery Megan wanted to run after him and explain that she'd just been generalizing, that there had been nothing personal in what she'd said, but it wouldn't be true. She'd been referring to the two of them and, judging from his reaction, he'd got the message.

The pity was that she hadn't said the rest of what was in her thoughts, mainly because she wasn't sure he would want to hear her say that if she hadn't been *his* first love, he had been *hers*, and nothing had changed regarding that.

In view of everything that was going on in the background, her timing had been atrocious, but he had insisted on pursuing the matter and she'd been honest with him, told him how she felt and made herself sound a lot of things she wasn't, such as smug, self-righteous and hard to please.

She didn't see him again for the rest of the afternoon and because her last patient of the day turned out to be a long consultation, by the time she was free, Luke had gone.

'Dr Anderson left a message to say he will see you in the morning. He's gone home to pick Owen up and then they're going back to the hospital,' Anne said when Megan surfaced, and she thought that he might be seeing her before that as she was anxious to see how Sue was coping.

But did she want to go to the hospital and butt in on them all, *and* have to endure Luke's coolness into the bargain? She had no doubt about how he'd construed what she'd said.

She decided to take the chance. Rather receive the cold shoulder from him than let the day end without seeing him again. Before she slept she needed to know just how much damage she'd done, and the only way to find out was face to face.

* * *

When Megan arrived on the ward Sue was nowhere to be seen, and she realised she should have phoned the house first. But Luke was there, observing her with dark, unreadable eyes as he looked up from the card game he was playing with the boys.

'I came to see Sue,' she told him, and felt that it sounded as if she was putting him in his place again.

'She's gone home to unpack her cases and have a rest,' he informed her levelly. 'So I'm afraid you've had a wasted journey.'

'Not at all. I came to visit Oliver, too,' she told him in a similar tone.

'He's doing fine, aren't you?' Luke asked his nephew. 'His hearing seems back to normal and the burns are healing nicely. He's going home tomorrow and then maybe we can all relax. Did Anne give you my message?'

'Yes. But I felt I had to see Sue. It was stupid of me not to ring the house first. My thinking wasn't very clear, was it?'

'I don't know about that. The last time we spoke, your thoughts were as clear as crystal.'

Megan could feel her colour rising as she told him, 'Not quite. Instead of explaining what I really meant, I got sidetracked.'

'It didn't sound like that to me.'

'No. Maybe not. But that's how it was. Luke, would you want me to be sparing with the truth?'

Owen was shuffling the cards and Oliver was fidgeting, anxious to get back to the game, so she said, 'I won't delay you. If the lights are on at Woodcote House I'll call to see Sue, and if they're not I'll be in touch, if you wouldn't mind passing on the message.'

'Of course not,' he said stiffly, and got up to walk to the door with her. 'Is there any news on Josh Meredith yet?' he asked as she stepped out into the corridor.

'Not so far. I'm going to call at the post office on my way home to see if Tom and Sara are back yet.'

'I'd be obliged if you would let me know if you hear anything.'

'Of course I will,' she said tartly. 'I'm surprised that you feel the need to ask. He's one of our patients, for heaven's sake.' Immediately sorry for being snappy, she added, 'How about Saturday for a ramble around my favourite places in the village? I'd really like to show you around as you haven't had much time to get to know it since you came.'

She was trying to make the peace but it wasn't working.

'I can't, I'm afraid,' he said stiffly. 'If you remember, I work in the garden centre at weekends.'

'Oh, yes, of course you do. It had slipped my mind. Some other time, then.'

'Maybe. But do you think it's a good idea?'

'What do you mean?'

'Megan, work it out for yourself. Surely I don't have to explain. You pointed out some things I wasn't aware of when we were by the riverbank in the lunch-hour.'

'Yes, I did, didn't I? And now I'm going to be punished for it, am I?'

He sighed. 'No. I shall just bear in mind what you said, that's all. We have to work together, don't forget.'

'I don't forget anything about *us*,' she told him, with tears sparkling on her lashes. He turned away to stop himself from taking hold of her and kissing them away. Megan was beautiful and unspoiled. He could understand why she didn't want to give her heart to a man who'd been married before and gone through a bitter divorce.

But she'd just been one of his students then. A girl who'd sent him a Valentine card, along with her friends. At the time he'd married Alexis he hadn't even known she existed, and if he had it would have made no difference. Teaching staff were not supposed to have relationships with students. And now he was discovering the hard way the difference between sexual attraction and real love.

'I'm going,' she said, brushing away the tears. 'We're going round in circles and getting nowhere.' She glanced at him. 'The boys are tired of waiting for you to go and finish the game. I'll see you in the morning, Luke.'

Staring straight ahead, she pointed herself

towards where she'd parked her car, and with a sigh Luke went to join his nephews.

There weren't any lights on at Woodcote House so it seemed that Sue had gone to bed after not having a moment to herself since she'd flown in from France.

As Oliver had seemed well enough, she presumed that Luke wouldn't stay the night this time and that soon he would bring Owen home, as it would be school again for him in the morning.

When she arrived at the post office Sara and Tom, looking totally exhausted, but happier than she'd seen them in a long time, had just arrived home.

'How did it go?' she asked.

'Good, so far, Megan,' Sara told her, 'You can see the difference in Josh already. He doesn't look as yellow, for one thing, and he's so grateful to have been given another chance. We know that it's early days yet, but we're hoping that the worst is over. He's had the transplant and, barring any hiccups, we can start looking forward.'

'That's wonderful!' Megan told them. She'd known these people since she'd been small. Since the days when she'd been barely tall enough to see what had been on the sweet counter and had taken ages to decide which of the penny treats she was going to buy. They were kind people and she was thankful that the fates were being kind to them in return.

She rang Luke on his mobile as soon as she arrived home and caught him on the point of leaving the hospital. 'It's good news from Sara and Tom,' she told him. 'Josh has had the surgery and according to them is looking better already.'

'That's great,' he said. 'I'm so pleased for them. Er, did you manage to see Sue?'

'No. All was in darkness so I didn't call. What are *your* plans for the evening?'

'Owen and I are ready to leave. Now that he's feeling better, Oliver says he doesn't need me to stay.'

'That's what I thought. I'm pleased that things at your end are sorting themselves out.'

There was silence at the other end of the

line and it was as if she could read his mind. 'Yes, it's great, isn't it,' he said flatly, and bade her goodbye.

The next morning everything was almost back to normal regarding the practice, but not with their own relationship. Luke was already behind his desk when Megan got there, engrossed in what was on the screen in front of him, and he said without looking up, 'Connie wants to have a word with me about her feet before she leaves to go to Woodcote House. There's an e-mail here from the orthopaedic consultant she's seen, and he's prepared to operate if she's willing, so I imagine that is what she wants to talk about.'

'It will be interesting to see what she decides,' Megan said, and thought that if they were going to be talking strictly shop she may as well log into her own computer and see what was happening to *her* patients.

She hoped that Connie would see the long-term benefits of the operation and if she decided to go ahead, arrangements would have to be made for her husband's care.

'Sue is picking Oliver up from the hospital this morning,' Luke said as she was about to depart. 'So I am now back on the job in the fullest sense. She is insisting that she will work in the garden centre this weekend and that I have some time to myself. So if your offer to show me the beauty spots of this rural paradise still stands, I would like to accept.'

He was telling himself that he was crazy. Why torture himself by being with Megan more than he had to? He could cope with being with her each day at the practice. There was no time for his feelings to run riot when they were there. It was health care from the moment they arrived to leaving at the end of the day, but spending hours together, just the two of them, would be a different matter.

He watched the face that was never out of his thoughts break into a smile and knew he didn't care. He just wanted to be with her. She was uncomplicated, and beautiful with it. If she didn't return his feelings, at least he would have had this time with her.

'Fine,' she said, as the October morning

suddenly seemed like spring. 'Do you want to make a day of it?'

'Yes. Why not? We can have lunch at some place that you recommend, and perhaps end the day with dinner somewhere. I feel as if I haven't come up for air since I came here, with Sue going to France so soon after I arrived, and coping with the antics of my two nephews. Maybe life will level out a bit now.'

'You are a kind and generous man,' she told him. 'Sue and the boys are lucky to have you.'

'And I'm fortunate to have them in *my* life, though I know you've had your doubts about that. They are all the family I've got. Or am ever likely to have, the way things are going.' He flashed her a quirky smile, 'But another day at the Riverside Practice beckons, I'm afraid.' Megan couldn't argue with that so she went to find out what, or who, was waiting for her attention.

That evening she phoned Sue and asked if she would like to come round for coffee. It would be easier to talk with just the two of them, she thought. Maybe her friend would open up to her more if they were alone, and when Sue said that she'd love to, it felt almost like old times. Almost, but not quite.

Things had changed. The boys seemed more settled in spite of the firework episode, and if the lads who had sold it to Owen and Oliver had come from their school, Luke would have been round there to investigate. But both his nephews had said they'd never seen them before. That they didn't live locally and they'd seen them getting off the train as if they'd come into the village from the town. It could have been so much worse, she thought thankfully, and now all they could do was hope that Sue's sons wouldn't do anything like that again.

When Sue arrived, Megan could see a difference in her friend. In spite of flying home to find her son in hospital, she looked brighter and more in charge. It was clear that a change of scene had done her a lot of good, and Megan thought that Luke had been right to let her go as he had.

'How is Oliver?' was Megan's first question, and his mother smiled.

'Home and happy to be so. Though I have a feeling that he quite enjoyed being in the lime-light for a short time and having the famous Alexis coming to see him twice. I suspect he enjoyed that more than Luke did.'

Megan smiled. 'You suspect right,' she said, and left it at that. There was no way she was going to pursue the subject of his ex-wife with his sister, but Sue wasn't aware that she had any reservations regarding Alexis and said, 'It was the biggest mistake Luke ever made. That woman broke his heart. Having seen him with my two, you'll know what a wonderful father he would make, but she put an end to that. I just hope that one day he'll find someone who will love, cherish him and give him the babies he longs for. And in the meantime, he's settling into village life like a natural. Now, tell me about yourself, Meg. How's life at the practice with my big brother sharing the load?'

'It's great,' Megan said. 'I'm taking him on a tour of all my favourite places on Saturday. He says that you're going to be available to help out at the garden centre so he's got some free time.'

She nodded 'Yes. I am. I feel ready to get a grip on things again. Luke has his own life to live and he isn't going to find his dream woman if he's bogged down with our affairs.'

Megan watched her friend leave a little later with mixed feelings. It was a great relief to see Sue more like her old self and ready to pick up the reins once more. But it was obvious that she didn't see her, Megan, as someone that Luke might fall in love with, and she thought wryly that although Alexis was a selfish and calculating woman, when it came to looks and style she was way ahead of herself. And in any case, if Luke *was* attracted to her, she'd already put a blight on that by telling him that he didn't have the right qualifications.

Why was life so complicated? she asked herself as she lay in her solitary bed, gazing out at a starlit sky. Why couldn't she have fallen in love with someone without so much emotional baggage?

* * *

She awoke on Saturday to a crisp, clear, morning and as she lay and let the pleasure of what lay ahead wash over her, Megan wondered if Luke was doing the same.

She didn't know why he'd changed his mind. On the face of it he'd done it because he had Saturday free now that Sue was home, but she didn't think that was it. Just as she hadn't been convinced that the garden centre was the real reason for his prompt refusal when she'd first asked him. A more likely reason was that he'd still been smarting at what she'd said about being the first love of the man she married.

She threw back the bedcovers resolutely and went to the window. Forget all that, she told herself. You have the chance of spending some quality time with Luke so make the best of it. Live one day at a time and see what *this* one brings.

They had arranged that he would drive up to the cottage, leave his car there and they would set off from that point, which left the moors the nearest place to introduce him to.

As he switched off the engine Megan came

out of the front door, and as Luke watched her lock it and turn to greet him he felt a tenderness inside him that was new and exhilarating. Alexis had never created the bone-melting feeling in him that was there every time he was with Megan. He wanted to cherish her, protect her, make love to her…if she would let him.

They were dressed the same in waterproof jackets, jeans and walking boots, hardly outfits to inspire romance, and quite unaware of the road that his thoughts were travelling along, Megan said, 'Just a mile further up the hill we come to the moors and it can be bleak up there. We haven't had any house calls from people living in those parts since you came, but that doesn't mean to say we won't.'

When they reached a plateau Luke took in the scene without speaking. All around them, rugged and tree-covered, the peaks stretched into the distance, separated from the moorland by deep gullies.

He looked down at the grass at his feet. It was long, dry and spiky. bent from continually being in the path of the winds that blew up there. It had none of the fresh green of the lawns and grass verges in the village and as she observed him questioningly he said wryly, 'You aren't telling me that this is one of your favourite places, surely.'

She smiled. 'It is in a way. I feel a sort of agelessness when I'm up here. It isn't always as bleak and lonely as it seems today. We get lots of walkers up here. There's a pub at the furthest point, which picks up reasonable trade according to weather conditions, and a farm not far away.'

It was his turn to smile. 'I'll bear that in mind if I'm called up here in winter. The pub, I mean, not the farm. So, where to now?'

'Civilisation. We go downwards, back towards the village, stopping at the youth hostel on the hillside, which is nearly always full. I used to work there in my teens for extra cash and the company before I went to university. I've had some great times there. It may not be your kind of place, having lived a much more sophisticated life than I have, but I did promise to show you *my* favourite places.'

'And am I complaining?'

He would have liked to tell her that sophistication could have its drawbacks, that her wholesome approach to life was cleansing and reassuring, but he had resolved that this day was not going to be spoilt by any comments rashly made that might make Megan retreat behind the barriers that had been there ever since their illuminating chat that day by the riverside.

The youth hostel *was* full, as she'd predicted, and he was impressed to see that now she was known to them as the local GP who they sent for when emergencies occurred, instead of the part-time helper of her teens.

When she'd introduced him to Mike and Angela, the middle-aged couple who were in charge of the place, and they'd accepted a mug of tea from them, Luke went around chatting to some of the young people there. Smiling, Mike nodded toward him and said, 'Your doctor friend is very much at ease with our visitors.'

'He was one of my lecturers when I was at university,' Megan told him. 'He's used to teenagers from then, and he now has two young nephews that he's keeping an eye on, who are a handful.'

'So what is he doing, working in a country practice?' Angela questioned.

'Luke's sister lives in the village. Her husband died not long ago and he's come to give her support.'

'And took the vacancy at the practice because he needed a job, I presume?'

'Yes. That more or less describes it.'

Luke came back to join them at that moment and said, 'Megan is taking me on a tour of all her favourite places today, and this is one of them.'

The husband-and-wife team laughed.

'Really?' Mike said. 'It's very nice of her to say so.' Turning to her, he said, 'And *you* were one of our favourite helpers, Megan. The lads were after her like bees around honey, weren't they, Angie?'

'Mmm,' Angela replied. 'They were, but our young helper was very choosy, weren't you?' she said, and Megan managed to dredge up a sick smile. She was squirming at the way the conversation was going. It was another instance of her sounding as if she put a high price on herself.

'I think we need to be going,' she said with outward calm, and then added with a smile that was completely genuine, 'It's been lovely to see you again. Thanks for the tea.'

'Why the rush?' Luke asked as they made their way down the hillside.

'I was embarrassed.'

'Why?'

'They said I was choosy.'

'Yes, they did. But I wasn't judging you, and neither were they.'

Megan sighed. 'Maybe, but it made me sound like someone who thinks she's something special.'

Dark brows were rising. 'No one is going to argue with that.' His voice deepened. 'It is what you are...special. Why do you think you were the only one I noticed in my class all that time ago? You weren't after every man who walked by. You wanted to qualify and that came first.'

'I did send you a Valentine, though.'

'Hmm, you did. It was the only one I took any notice of once I'd recognised your writing.'

'And you didn't exactly fall over yourself with excitement, if I remember rightly.'

'There were two reasons for that. Both equally stressing. I was still married at the time *and* smarting, I might tell you, though my divorce was going through. And I would never have entered into a relationship with a student. It would have been against protocol and my own principles. But, Megan, let's forget the past. Make the most of the present and enjoy the day.'

'Yes, of course,' she agreed quickly. 'That was my intention. I let myself get sidetracked by what Mike and Angela said and promise not to let it happen again. So forward to our next stopping place.'

'Which is?'

'Elevenses with Aunt Izzy.'

He groaned. 'You're joking.'

'Yes, I am,' she admitted sweetly. 'We're going to stop for coffee in the heart of the village. The Goyt Gallery behind the church

does light refreshments besides selling paintings. Sonia Clayborne who owns it is an artist
herself. Over the years she's painted me a few
times. She says that my colouring comes up
well on canvas.'

'When was the last time?' he asked, immediately tuned in.

'Recently. Since I've come back to live in the
village. I did some sittings for her before you
came, but don't know if the portrait is finished.
I've never been keen on having my face on
view in the gallery, but Sonia is a sweet old
thing and very talented, so I give in when she
asks me to sit for her.'

'So that's why we are calling there, to see if
it's finished?'

Megan shook her head. 'No, of course not. I
want your opinion. Sonia isn't at all well, but
getting her to come to the surgery is like getting
blood out of a stone. She thinks she is in-
vincible, that ill health isn't going to come her
way, but she's wrong. I feel it has already
arrived and I want to know what you think
when you see her.'

'Sure,' he said easily. 'Anything to oblige the friend of a friend. But am I going to be able to tell by just looking?'

'I don't know. But you have a lot more experience than I have.'

They swung on to the main street of the village and she pointed to where the ancient church stood that dated back to Norman times. 'The gallery is behind in a small cul-de-sac.'

'So which comes first,' he asked whimsically, 'the coffee or the covert consultation?'

'How about simultaneously?'

'Of course,' he agreed.

The first thing Luke was aware of as they entered the small but elegant gallery was that the portrait *was* finished. It dominated the centre of the room on a large easel and it was so lifelike it took his breath away.

The artist had captured Megan's clear-eyed gaze on the world and her striking colouring at the same time, and his heartbeat quickened. But his companion's gaze was on the woman who had appeared from behind a heavy velvet curtain at the back of the shop. She hadn't even noticed the portrait.

'Sonia,' she said. 'This is my colleague, Dr Anderson. I've been telling him about the gallery and he's come to look at your paintings as he is very interested in art of any kind.'

The woman observing him with bright birdlike eyes was not young. Sixties or early seventies, he would have thought. She was painfully thin—gaunt, in fact, with arms and legs like sticks and dark skin around the eyes, but it seemed that there was nothing wrong with her mind.

'Good morning, Dr Anderson,' she said briskly. 'It is a pleasure to meet you. Though I doubt we shall be seeing much of each other unless you come to buy a painting.'

I *shall* be wanting to buy a painting, he thought, and unless I'm very much mistaken you are going to be seeing quite a lot of me.

It was not a thought that he was going to pass on to her at the moment of meeting, so he just smiled. Sonia turned to Megan, who was gazing open-mouthed at the portrait, and said, 'So what do you think of it, Meg o' mine.'

'Is that really me?' Megan breathed.

Sonia smiled. 'None other, and, though I say it, I think it's the best thing I've ever done. It's taken me a while because I'm always tired these days, but with the coffee-shop and this place, I suppose it isn't surprising.'

'So maybe it's time you paid the Riverside Practice a visit,' Megan said gently. 'You might need a tonic or something of the sort.'

This lady was going to need more than a tonic, Luke thought. He'd seen people like her before who ignored the signs to the point of collapse and then they had to accept treatment whether they wanted it or not, and sometimes it was too late. But he was not going to stick his oar in at that moment.

He couldn't stop looking at the portrait. Megan had sat for it in a strapless dress of emerald brocade and as he gazed at the smooth lines of her shoulders and the hollow between her breasts he felt raw desire inside him for the first time in many long months and this time, mixed with it, was the tenderness that she aroused in him whenever they were together.

Aware of how intently he was observing it, Megan had turned away with rising colour and was saying to Sonia, 'We've called for a coffee and one of Barbara's delicious cakes.'

Barbara was a friend of Sonia's who served in the coffee-shop and made the cakes and scones on sale there.

While they were being served, Sonia was called back into the shop and Barbara said hurriedly, 'You doctors have got to make Sonia see sense. I feel as if she's dying before my eyes.'

Megan nodded, her expression grave. 'That's why I've brought Dr Anderson in on the pretext of a coffee. I need his opinion. We can't discuss it here, Barbara, but once we've left he will tell me what he thinks and we'll take it from there.'

'She does need help,' Luke said in a low voice, 'and some persuasion may be needed, but the lady needs to be treated fast if she wants to carry on with her painting and whatever else she does.'

At that moment Sonia came back and while Megan chatted to Barbara he said to her, 'I'd love to have a stroll around the gallery if you could spare the time to show me what you have for sale.'

'Of course,' she said immediately, and the moment they were out of earshot he said, 'I want to buy the portrait of Megan. Will you put it to one side for me? I'll come to collect it the first chance I get. Please, don't tell her I've bought it, will you? I want it to be a surprise when I tell her.'

'I'd like it to go to someone who cares for her,' Sonia said. 'To a friend, or family.'

'It will be,' he told her with strengthening determination. 'You can rely on that.'

CHAPTER SEVEN

'SO WHAT do you think is wrong with Sonia?' Megan asked as soon as they were out of sight of the gallery.

'It could be anaemia, due to an iron deficiency, or further along the line than that, cancer of the liver or the colon,' said Luke. 'That is only guessing, but I've seen this sort of thing before, as I'm sure you have.'

She nodded. 'That's what I thought, but I needed to hear your opinion. So how do we get her to have treatment? She needs blood tests before anything else, and I know what she'll say.'

'To you maybe, but how about I have a go at persuading her? There shouldn't be any delay or it might be too late. I'll call round tomorrow on some sort of pretext and do the blood tests while I'm there. She won't expect me to be wearing my doctor's hat on a Sunday morning.'

'If she'll agree.'

Luke's voice was reassuringly firm. 'She'll agree. I shall charm her into it if all else fails. Your favourite places are certainly not what I expected. The bleak, windswept moors, a youth hostel and now a picture gallery. What next?'

'I used to go to Sonia's place when I was a child,' Megan explained. 'She always had time to talk to me and feed me. My mum and dad were always so busy. I used to sit and watch her paint for hours. I was surprised when I saw my portrait. I didn't notice it at first because I was looking at Sonia, dreading that she might have lost more weight. What did you think of it?'

What did he think of it? He would love to tell her that he was going to buy it, but it might cause her to withdraw from him. She might feel he was overstepping the mark.

There was a pond in the middle of the village green and as they walked beside it a couple of plump ducks came waddling up, expecting bread, but soon lost interest when none was forthcoming.

'If only life could be as uncomplicated as theirs,' Luke said. 'Bread, or no bread, and a noisy quack, quack.'

'You haven't answered my question,' Megan said, as they left the hungry birds behind.

'I think the portrait is excellent,' he said, hoping he sounded casual. 'Your friend Sonia is very talented. It is up to you and I to see that she lives to paint another day, so we'll see what tomorrow brings.'

And now can we do something that involves just the two of us? he was thinking, and almost as if she'd read his mind Megan said, 'After lunch we'll explore the river bank, my most favourite place of all, if that's all right with you.'

'Of course,' he said, and thought with grim amusement that a tour of the places that appealed to Alexis would include the top hotels, smart restaurants, boutiques, all very nice in their own way, but froth compared to the real things of life. While to Megan, the people and places she was introducing him to had been part of the secure idyll of her youth and were just as precious now in adulthood.

On the Valentine card that she'd sent him all that time ago she'd written that she was attracted to him. He prayed that was still the case. That she'd chosen to spend this day with him because she felt the same as he did.

They had lunch at The Badger and then strolled down to the riverside, and as they passed the solid stone building that was the surgery Anne, who lived in the apartment above, came out and looked at them in surprise.

'Megan is taking me on a guided tour of the village,' he said easily, 'in case I decide to take up permanent residence here.'

'Ah! I see,' she replied.

I wish *I* did, Megan thought with a sinking feeling inside her. Luke had said right from the start that he wanted to live in the village. That when his sister's life was on a more stable footing he would buy a place of his own, but now he didn't sound so sure, and she hoped that she wasn't the reason why.

They were on the riverbank now, walking

along on a carpet of bronze and gold that had been the green leaves of summer. Turning to face him, she said, 'So it isn't definite that you're going to stay in the village. You aren't so entranced with it after all.'

Luke turned away to avoid her seeing his expression and said lightly, 'Yes, I am. I think it is an enchanting place, but I could live at the foot of a coal tip, or next to a railway line, and be happy if I was there with the right person.

'I've learnt a lesson that I won't forget in a hurry with regard to human relationships and freely admit that I've no one to blame but my own faulty judgement. It is a poor marriage when a wife conceals the fact that she is pregnant from her husband because she doesn't want his child.'

They'd been strolling along at a leisurely pace, but now Megan halted abruptly, and as he observed her questioningly she said tightly, 'Stop! I don't want to hear any more. What Alexis did was awful, but there are lots of decent women in the world. If you look hard enough you'll find one.'

He was staring at her, aghast.

'What has brought this on, might I ask?'

Megan sighed. 'Sue wants you to find your dream woman, so maybe you'd better start looking.'

'Maybe I had,' he said frostily, 'and I hope they won't all be as choosey as someone I know, who makes no bones about *her* criteria.'

Choosy, am I? Megan thought tearfully, with the pain of listening to him describe his marriage like a knife in her heart. Luke doesn't know that I made my choice long ago without realising it. Can't he see that? And with the need for an answer to the question she stepped up to him and placing her arms around his neck, kissed him long and lingeringly on the mouth.

She felt him go slack with surprise and then he was kissing her back like a hungry man at a banquet, and as his arms tightened around her she thought that this was what she'd been waiting for.

But she'd had to be the one to make the first move and even as she faced up to that knowledge, Luke's arms were slackening, his kiss no longer holding her spellbound.

'I vowed that there would be none of this today,' he said, putting her away from him gently, 'much as I could go on kissing you for ever. But I've told myself I will respect what you said regarding me having been married before, and will not take advantage of you in any way.'

Megan had gone very pale. It wasn't exactly a rebuff that Luke was handing out, but it was a message loud and clear that she wasn't the only one with boundaries.

'So, are we going to carry on with our tour of the riverbank,' he was asking quietly, 'or have you had enough of me for one day?'

She would never have enough of him, she thought achingly. He was the answer to all her hopes and dreams, but where before *she'd* been hesitant about their relationship, now *he* was the one putting up barriers and she was going to have to accept it.

'We'll carry on if that's what you want,' she told him flatly, 'and forget my error of judgement, if that's all right with you.'

It wasn't all right with him at all, he thought. He was the one who'd turned it into a lost opportunity. But at least she was still there, hadn't gone storming off, like a lot of women would have done.

Taking her by surprise, he said, 'Yes, it's fine by me, and as you aren't going to desert me, I'll race you to the bridge that I see in the distance.'

'Right,' she agreed, managing a smile, and before he'd got his breath she was off, moving fast in spite of the walking boots to where an old iron bridge spanned the river.

He was only a foot behind her but Megan was there first and as she collapsed breathlessly against its ancient frame, her world was righting itself. She'd almost spoilt the day by losing control, but Luke had an answer for everything.

He was observing the structure of the bridge and commenting that it looked a bit rickety. 'Yes, it is,' she agreed. 'It's going to cost thousands to repair.' She pointed to the land beside the river. 'That is parkland. Lots of people walk their dogs along it, or just come for a stroll, and this old bridge is dear to their hearts. A committee has been formed to raise funds for its repair and the first event to take place is a ball at the beginning of December at Beresford Lodge, the hotel that you pass on the way to the tops.'

'Sounds good. Am I going to take you?'

'Maybe. Unless I get a better offer,' she told him laughingly, knowing there couldn't possibly be a better offer than that. She was rallying from the aftermath of the kiss. Telling herself that it wasn't all gloom. She knew now that Luke wanted her as much as she wanted him. He'd said he could have gone on kissing her for ever. Yet the fact remained that he hadn't. If she found herself in his arms again, it would be of his doing, not hers.

They turned back at the bridge because the light was fading and the birds and animals of the riverbank were no longer to be seen. As the surgery came into view again Luke said, 'So are we going to go home to change, and finish the day off with dinner? That was the plan, if I remember rightly.'

She hesitated for a moment and then asked, 'Are you sure that Sue and the boys won't need you this evening? I know that she seems to be back on top of things, but it won't always be the case.'

'Megan, I'm aware of that,' he protested, 'and will take care to see that I'm always there if she needs me. Are you sure that you aren't using Sue as an excuse not to have dinner with me?'

'I might be. I'm not sure whether I am or not.'

'Perhaps you're thinking that it's been a long day and enough is enough.'

Now it was her turn to protest. 'I'm not thinking anything of the kind. I'd love to have dinner with you.'

'Good. So why don't we go to this Beresford Lodge place. We've had coffee amongst culture and a lunch of pub grub, so I think it's only fitting if we hit the high spots for dinner. Shall I reserve a table?'

'Yes,' she agreed, already debating what she was going to wear.

'I'll pick you up about eightish, if that's all right with you, but first I'm going to walk you home and pick up my car.'

As Megan dressed for what she wished was a date rather than just two friends dining together, she passed over a smart black dress that she'd bought recently for a more sophisticated image and chose the dress she'd worn for the portrait, quite unaware of the impression it had made on Luke. She was recalling what he'd said about sophistication, and the last thing she wanted was to appear looking like a watered-down clone of his ex-wife. Of all things she wanted him to see her as herself.

When she opened the door to him just before eight o'clock he said, 'That's the dress you wore for the painting, isn't it?'

'Er…yes.' She was taken aback that he'd remembered. 'Do you approve?'

'Of course I do.'

'I think both of our outfits are an improvement on what we did the village tour in,' she said, smiling across at the tall figure on her doorstep who was dressed in a dark suit, smart shirt and tie.

Luke took her hand and led her down the steps. 'So off we go, then.' He then diminished the promise of the moment by going on, 'Two hard-working doctors let off the leash for once.'

'Yes,' she agreed flatly, and thought how much she would have liked him to be able to describe them as lovers rather than busy GPs. But the afternoon's episode had set a pattern of behaviour and Luke seemed to be intent on keeping to it.

The dining room at Beresford Lodge was full, it being Saturday, and as they were shown to a table for two by a window Megan looked around her. She'd dined there before a couple of times with Sue, but since then it had been refurbished. Observing the elegance of the place, it seemed to have been well worth the expense.

'This will make a perfect place for a Christmas ball. Especially if the organisers decide it should be fancy dress to a festive theme,' Luke said when they were seated. 'You could be the fairy on the Christmas tree and I could be Ebenezer Scrooge.'

She was smiling at him across the table. 'I can't think of anyone less fitted for either part. Me as a fairy and you, the kindest of men, as Scrooge.'

'You ain't seen the worst side o' me yet, missy,' he quipped back.

She loved this man, Megan thought. It would be enchantment to spend the rest of her days with him. When she'd known him before he'd been the reserved lecturer who'd snubbed her Valentine card and maybe it was as well that he had.

She'd been in love with love in those days, and once she'd graduated had almost forgotten the only man she'd ever been attracted to. Almost, but not quite. There'd never been anyone else who'd made her bones melt or her heart beat faster at the mere sight of them.

When Sue had told her that Luke had been married and was now divorced, she'd accepted it calmly enough on the outside, but deep down she'd been hurting. Yet had she really expected that someone with his looks and standing wouldn't have tried the marriage game by then?

Thinking of Sue brought her back to the present and she asked, 'Was everything all right at Woodcote House when you got home?'

'Yes. The boys had gone to the birthday party of one of Owen's friends and Sue was winding down after a day in the garden centre. As you can imagine, the demand for growing things reduces as winter sets in and she was wondering whether to close until nearer Christmas.'

'What did you say?'

'I said don't do it. Put up with dwindling sales rather than close. Once the public get used to a business being shut they don't take the trouble to go back when it opens again because they've found somewhere else to shop. I've suggested that we make a really big splash at Christmas with trees, ornaments and so on, and maybe open a small café on the premises.'

'And what did she say?'

'Thought it was a good idea.'

'So do I,' she told him, 'and I can see the reasoning behind it, apart from the money angle. If she's kept busy, it will be easier for her to get through their first Christmas without Gareth.'

'You read my mind,' he said sombrely.

At that moment the food they'd ordered arrived and as they were both hungry after the day's other activities silence fell as they enjoyed the catering of Beresford Lodge.

It was not to last. The manager made a hurried appearance and asked urgently, 'Dr Marshall, please, could you help us?'

Luke put down his knife and fork and got to his feet, and Megan did the same. 'We are both doctors,' he told him. 'What's the problem?'

'Will you come this way, please?' the manager asked, lowering his voice. When they were out of earshot of the other diners he said, 'A visitor has been found unconscious in one of the bedrooms. I've sent for an ambulance but thought if there was a doctor present they could perhaps attend to her until it arrives.'

'Of course,' Luke replied. 'We will do what

we can.' As he flashed her a wry smile Megan thought that this was going to be an imperfect ending to an imperfect day.

The woman lying on the thick carpeting in a second-floor bedroom was indeed uncon-scious. Middle-aged, and dressed in just a long cotton robe, she seemed to have been carrying a bag of toiletries as it was on the floor beside her with the contents strewn around it.

A chambermaid and the assistant manager were with her when they arrived, both trying to rouse her but without success. As the two doctors knelt beside her Megan said, 'She hasn't got the bluish tinge to the lips or the clammy skin of a cardiac arrest.'

'No, indeed,' he agreed, as they checked the breathing and pulse.

'Do you think she's taken something?' she questioned.

'There's a strip of tablets that looks like pre-scribed medication on the bedside table,' the chambermaid said. 'I noticed them when I came in to turn the bedcovers down.'

She went to get them and handed them to Megan who informed him. 'They're beta-blockers, Luke.'

'Hmm. Those little fellows can be tricky under certain circumstances. They do the job in lots of cases, but I've known a few people who've had a bad reaction to them.'

Megan was looking down at the packet in her hand. 'I've prescribed these for migraine and over active thyroid and had no bad reports.'

'So have I,' he agreed, 'but there is always the one person who they don't suit and then we are in big trouble.'

The woman on the carpet moaned softly at that moment and then opened her eyes. 'What happened?' she asked muzzily. 'Did I faint?'

'We don't know,' Megan told her gently. 'What are you taking the tablets for?'

'Migraine, asthma, anxiety, lots of things.'

'Has anything like this happened before?' Luke asked.

'I've felt odd a few times, but I've never collapsed before. I was getting ready to go down for dinner and that's the last I remember. I'm here with my firm. It's a sort of staff getting to know each other weekend. They'll be wondering where I am.'

She was trying to sit up and Megan said, 'The manager has sent for an ambulance. Just stay where you are for the moment.'

'I don't want to go to hospital,' the woman said tearfully. 'I'm all right now.'

'You didn't collapse for no reason,' Luke told her gently. 'You need to be checked over. It could be your tablets that caused it, or some other problem, and they'll deal with that in A and E.'

Their patient nodded meekly. 'I suppose you're right.' She looked up at the faces of those gathered around her. 'You've been very kind. My name is Helen Somerfield. If someone could tell my boss what's happened, I'd be grateful. Though they'll all be halfway through their dinner by now. I don't want to disturb them.'

'I'll go with Mrs Somerfield, if it's all right with you,' the chambermaid said to the manager.

'Yes, by all means,' he agreed, anxious to ensure the situation was dealt with as quickly as possible. 'And as you could be there some time, take the day off tomorrow.'

The ambulance had taken the dazed woman to hospital, and now the two doctors were about to take up where they'd left off. Their table had been reset, with a bottle of champagne on ice in a central position, and staff were waiting to serve them with a freshly cooked meal to replace the one they'd had to leave in such a hurry.

As the wine waiter poured the champagne he said, 'Compliments of the manager.'

When he'd gone Luke said whimsically, 'The trouble with doctors is they can never escape their profession. Has it spoilt your evening, Megan?'

She shook her head. 'No, of course not.' It was true. They'd been doing what they'd been trained to do… together…and it had been a great feeling. There were no unclear agendas when it came to the job.

If the rest of their lives were progressing as smoothly she would be up in the clouds. But although they were two people in the grip of a strong attraction, they were also unevenly balanced when it came to lifestyles.

Her life was clear and uncluttered, she thought, while Luke's was bulging at the seams with family responsibilities and a past relationship that kept rearing its head.

She'd always imagined that falling in love would be simple. That she would meet the man of her dreams, who would have the same feelings, and the romance would move on from there. The last thing she'd expected was having to cope with following in someone else's footsteps. Even though Luke had made it clear that the only feelings left over from his marriage were hurt and anger.

When they arrived back at the cottage it was way past midnight and as she was about to invite him in for a drink, Luke said, 'As we drove past I noticed that there seemed to be still a lot of activity at the house where the boys have been invited to a party, so if you don't mind I'll make tracks. It is too late for youngsters of their age to be partying.'

He touched her cheek fleetingly. 'It's been a strange day, hasn't it, Megan? Full of highs and lows, and just because I called a halt, don't be thinking that what happened on our way to the iron bridge wasn't the highest point.' He smiled. 'Lock up when I've gone. Sleep well. And wish me luck with your friend Sonia tomorrow.'

Megan nodded without speaking, understanding what he'd said about his nephews but not wanting him to go. It *had* been the kind of day he'd described. Amongst the good parts had been lost chances.

They knew each other well enough as doctors, but getting to know each other as people was another matter, and after she'd watched the taillights of Luke's car disappear into the night she went slowly up to bed.

When he called at the home of Owen's friend, Luke discovered that it was the adults who were partying at that hour after the youngsters had gone home, and he breathed a sigh of relief on that score. The last thing he'd wanted was to do the heavy uncle act.

They were both fast asleep when he looked in on them and no sounds were coming from his sister's room. So in the quiet house he stripped out of the clothes he'd worn for the evening with Megan and lay on top of the covers, gazing out into the night.

He knew that she hadn't wanted him to go and he'd felt the same. But his feeling of responsibility for the boys hadn't gone away with the return of their mother. It could easily have been a houseful of unsupervised young people partying in the house on the main street of the village.

His last thoughts before sleep were of that kiss. It would have been so easy to take it further, but he wasn't going to let Megan get carried away when she had reservations about him. While those remained, the future was uncertain and he was not going to cause her any grief.

He went round to the Gallery before it was due to open the next morning. The last thing he wanted was to discuss Sonia's health with her in the front of other people, except for the faithful Barbara, who was carrying in a big wooden tray that contained cakes and scones when he arrived.

'Have you come to persuade Sonia to get her health sorted?' she asked, 'Or is it Megan's portrait you've come for? Sonia told me you were interested.'

'I've come because of both,' he told her. 'Regarding Sonia, I've even brought my medical kit with me so that if she agrees to have blood tests, I can do them on the spot. If they are left until the surgery opens tomorrow, she could have changed her mind by then, but first of all I've got to get her to agree to have them. I'm afraid if she doesn't, the surgery won't be able to answer for the consequences. Anyone can see that she's a sick woman.'

'Except Sonia herself,' Barbara commented.

'Hmm. That happens a lot. Just as some people think they're ill when they're not.'

'I'll stay out of the way,' Barbara told him. 'Sonia won't want an audience.'

When Sonia saw him, the gallery owner said,

'You're an early bird, Dr Anderson. I take it that you've come for Megan's portrait.'

'Yes,' he said easily, 'and one other thing.'

'And what might that be?'

'Two people who care for you a lot are very worried about your health, Sonia.'

She groaned. 'Oh, not that again. I'm all right.'

'I think we might have to differ on that. I'd like to take some blood tests, if you agree. Megan tells me that you've lost a lot of weight, have no appetite and are tired all the time.'

'That happens to lots of people.'

'Yes, it does, and in some cases it is just a temporary thing. In others it is a warning that something serious is the cause. But we aren't going to find out if that is the case without blood tests. So, if you would just roll up your sleeve?'

For a moment it seemed as if Sonia might refuse and then with a sigh she did as he'd asked. 'Have you had a bad experience with the medical profession that you are so reluctant to seek help?' he asked as he tightened the strap around a bony arm.

'No, not with them. I nursed my mother with

cancer of the colon, and as it progressed she looked just like I do, skin and bone. I've had other relatives with the same thing and now I feel that it's my turn.'

'And you aren't prepared to do anything about it.'

'What's the point?'

'The point is that it may not be cancer, and if it is, treatments are so advanced these days it doesn't mean that it will be fatal. So shall we see what the bloods I've taken tell us before we jump to any conclusions?'

'Yes, all right,' Sonia said listlessly, 'and bear in mind that Megan is not to blame for any of this. She has tried repeatedly to get me to go to the surgery.'

'Of course,' he said calmly. 'She is a good doctor *and* a good friend. The results of the tests should be back from the lab in two to three days. As soon as I've got them I'll give you a call. And now to my other reason for being here, the portrait.'

'Why do you want it? You haven't been here long enough to know her that well.'

'I know Megan from way back. She was a student of mine at university,' he explained, 'and the moment I saw it I realised it had been painted by a very talented artist.'

He wasn't going to explain that he was in love with her.

'I've painted her many times over the years,' Sonia told him, 'and maybe I put everything I had into this one because I felt it was going to be my last.'

'Yes, well, we'll have to see about that,' he said gently. 'You've made a step in the right direction by letting me take the bloods and we'll take it from there.'

He rang Megan when he got back to Woodcote House to tell her that he'd done the blood tests and she said, 'Oh, thank goodness!'

'Sonia's reluctance to seek medical help is because she thinks she's got terminal cancer,' he explained. 'Apparently her mother died from the illness and so have other relatives. It is almost as if she's been expecting it and has just gone along with it. She might be right, of course, but not necessarily. There are other causes for severe weight loss, but we'll just have to wait and see.'

'I'm so relieved that you got through to her,' she told him. 'When Sonia decides on something, she doesn't usually change her mind, like someone else I know. And now tell me what happened about the boys last night. *Had* the party got out of hand?'

'No. The youngsters had all gone home. It was the parents living it up. So much for jumping to conclusions. I needn't have rushed off like I did.'

'You only did what you thought was right,' she told him with a flatness to her voice. 'You're good at that, aren't you? Preventing situations from getting out of hand.'

'What is that supposed to mean?'

'I think you know,' she told him in the same flat tone.

There was silence for a moment and then his voice came over the line, cool and controlled. 'Maybe I do. But I'm not the person who creates those same situations, am I? I rang to tell you about Sonia, not to become involved in a war of words, Megan. Enjoy what's left of your weekend. I'll see you tomorrow.' And as the line went dead she went back to the pile of ironing that she'd been working through before Luke had phoned.

CHAPTER EIGHT

As THE amount of ironing decreased, Megan's annoyance with herself increased. Why had she been so prickly with Luke? she asked herself. It was wonderful that he'd persuaded her stubborn friend Sonia to let him take blood tests, and his leaving in a rush the night before had been because it had been part of the task he'd set himself, looking after his fatherless nephews.

She'd had him all to herself yesterday, had had his full attention. So why wasn't she satisfied with that, instead of feeling that Luke was there for everyone and she was just one of many?

It had been a day to remember, but the time they'd spent together hadn't all been happy. There'd been his sombre rebuff when she'd kissed him and the crisis at Beresford Lodge when they'd had their meal interrupted by the manager.

It had felt good, the two of them being involved in treating the sick woman, but when they'd returned to the dining room the promise of the evening had disappeared.

His life was so full. Compared to it, hers was empty, she thought. She'd been content before he'd come back into her life. Seen the way ahead clearly, with her eventually falling in love with someone of a similar mind to herself and continuing to enjoy country life as she'd always done. But Luke wasn't the only one who could be happy living at the side of a railway line as long as she was with the right man.

She knew what had prompted him to say such a thing. He'd made one big mistake and wasn't going to make another. While for her part she was still trying to come to terms with his past. Not a good recipe for contentment for either of them.

When she'd put the ironing board away she decided to get out of the cottage. Go for a walk along the tops. Then have lunch at The Badger…again.

There was a strong wind blowing when she reached the moors and unlike the day before there was a chill in the air that said summer had finally gone. Yet there were quite a few people up there. Walkers, and older folk eating their packed lunches inside the warmth of their cars as they admired the views.

As she strode along with her head bent against the wind and hands deep in her coat pockets, she heard her name called, and when she looked round Luke and the boys were approaching from behind, flying a large kite.

'Where are you off to?' he asked when they drew level.

'Nowhere in particular,' she told him. 'I came for some fresh air and thought I'd have lunch while I'm out.'

Just the sight of him was banishing the blues. He looked fit and in charge, like he always did, in a leather jacket and jeans. As the wind ruffled the dark thatch of his hair she wanted to reach out and touch him, but Luke had other things on his mind.

'Do you mind if we join you?' he asked. 'It

will save me cooking. Sue and Ned have gone to the warehouse to buy the Christmas stock. We're hoping to make a big splash this time. Trees, fresh and artificial, fairy-lights, ornaments, toys and things, and we're opening a small café to bring in extra trade. So hopefully it's going to be a busy time.'

'We're even having Father Christmas. I've been roped in for that as it was my idea. How about you assisting me as the Christmas fairy?'

'I think not,' she told him laughingly.

'Why? A tinsel topping on that beautiful hair of yours would be riveting.'

'I remember you suggested me as a fairy before, but in connection with the Christmas ball at Beresford Lodge. On that occasion you saw yourself as someone less likeable than Santa Claus.'

'Ebenezer Scrooge, you mean? I can be very versatile, you know.'

'You don't have to convince me of that,' she said wryly. 'I've seen you in action.' Her voice cooled. 'But what about the practice? Are you contemplating doing both at once? Handing out the goodies and treating the patients at the same time beside the bran tub.'

Luke was frowning. 'No, of course not. I know that you have only one priority in your life and it's the practice. I am not going to neglect my responsibilities there to be Santa Claus. I shall only be doing it at weekends, Saturdays and Sundays. Does that satisfy you?'

'Yes,' she said lamely, feeling like the local killjoy. When an alternative to eating at The Badger appeared in the distance she said, 'We could have lunch at The Moorend if you like. Do you remember me telling you there was a pub up here on the moors? Well, it's just ahead of us.'

'Suits me, and the lads will eat anywhere.'

The Moorend came a long way behind Beresford Lodge in elegance, but it did have its own atmosphere, with stags' heads mounted on the walls and log fires in huge black fireplaces with brass fenders.

But to Owen and Oliver the most interesting part of the place was a railway carriage of a bygone age situated on land at the back, and for a while the kite was relegated to second best in things of interest.

Inside the railway carriage was an exhibition of paintings by local artists, a reminder of the portrait he had bought that morning, which was now concealed in his bedroom until such time as he had a place of his own. He didn't want it on view as Sue might start asking questions that he didn't have answers to.

When they'd eaten of food that was plentiful but unimaginative, and were ready to make the return journey, there was a leaden sky above and thunder was rumbling in the distance.

'What do you suggest we do?' Luke said. 'Stay put, or set off and risk a soaking? You know these parts much better than I do, Megan.'

'A soaking wouldn't be the end of the world,' she told him, 'but if the mists come down, as they sometimes do, without any warning, it can be dangerous.'

'So as I am responsible for Owen and Oliver it would seem that the best thing to do is wait until the storm has passed.'

'Mmm, and what do we do in the meantime?'

'You and I can sit by the fire and relax, and I thought I saw a chessboard when we came in. It's a game that the boys are into, so that could keep them occupied for a while. I'm sure that the landlord won't mind, as they do seem to cater for children here.'

The storm when it came was frightening. Thunder rumbled noisily overhead and forked lightning lit up the dark sky every few moments.

Megan shuddered. The palms of her hands were moist, but her mouth was dry and her heartbeat was booming in her ears. Shortly after she'd begun working in the practice she'd done a home visit to a patient living in a remote cottage not far from The Moorend, and on her way back to the practice had been caught in a storm such as this. As she'd driven carefully through heavy rain and in semi-darkness a large tree that had been struck by lightning had fallen sideways onto her car.

Fortunately the roof had held the weight of the branches long enough for her to scramble out into the storm, exchanging one moment of terror for another as she had become drenched in the heavy downpour, while thunder had continued to crash around overhead and lightning flashed too near for comfort.

When she'd been late back her father had set out to look for her and found her crouching beside one of the dry stone walls that divided the rugged landscape, unhurt but traumatised by being exposed to the elements out of control. There hadn't been a major storm since then, and it had brought the horror of that other time with it.

Luke had seen her shudder and he questioned, 'What is it, Megan? You don't like this?'

She shook her head and cringed as a vivid blue flash danced along one of the fluorescent tubes behind the bar and all the power went off. Fortunately there was still some degree of daylight and Luke got up from his seat at the other side of the log fire and, seating himself beside her, put his arms around her.

'You're trembling,' he said gently as she buried her head against his chest. 'This is some storm, but it will pass. Places like this usually have their own generator to fall back on in emergencies, so we should have some power back on soon.'

He was stroking her hair, overcome with tenderness yet surprised that she was in such a state. But he supposed that it took all sorts of things to scare all sorts of people. Like spiders, mice or needles, to name a few. He'd seen strong men turn pale when they had to have an injection or give blood.

But it was the first time he'd ever seen Megan not in control. Or, come to think of it, maybe it was the second. There'd been the kiss that had come out of the blue. What had triggered that he didn't know, but he wished he'd handled it better.

As Megan stayed in the safe circle of his arms she was thinking that Luke must be wondering where her panic was coming from. A storm was a storm. Something that came and went, but it was too close for reassurance.

If *she* was afraid and Luke puzzled, the boys were neither of those things. Owen and Oliver were enjoying the thrill of the lights going out and the violence of the storm. It had taken precedence over the railway carriage and the kite.

They were edging towards the door and Luke said calmly, 'Don't even think about it. You will be soaked in seconds if you go out there and the lightning is too close for safety.'

He felt Megan shudder again and held her closer. At that moment the lights came back on, and he hoped she would feel less afraid.

Having been forbidden to go outside, Owen and Oliver were turning their attention to Megan. Oliver, always first with a question, asked, 'What's wrong with Dr Marshall? Is she sick?'

Luke shook his head. 'No. Just a bit overwhelmed by the storm, that's all.'

'You mean she's scared,' the boy hooted.

'We all have things that spook us, Oliver. Isn't it you that's afraid of going to the dentist?'

'Yes, but…'

The landlord's wife was going around snuffing out the candles that had been hurriedly lit when the power had gone, and she stopped beside them. 'Isn't the lady young Dr Marshall from the practice in the village?' she asked, and Megan lifted her head.

'Yes. That's me,' she said in surprise.

'So why don't you tell this young fellow what happened to you the last time we had something like this?'

Megan shook her head, but Luke wasn't letting that pass. 'Tell me, Megan. I need to know what it is that you're frightened of.'

'Shortly after I joined the practice I was caught in a dreadful storm after visiting a patient not far from here,' she said reluctantly. 'A tree was struck by lightning and it fell onto my car. I managed to get out safely and then found myself in the middle of nowhere with thunder and lightning all around me and nowhere to shelter. My dad came looking for me eventually and took me home to safety, but my car was a write-off and I've dreaded being caught in another storm ever since.'

She moved out of Luke's arms and, looking up at him, she said quietly, 'I'm sorry to have made such a fuss.'

'And I'm sorry for what I said, Dr Marshall,' Oliver said sheepishly.

She threw him a pale smile. 'You weren't to know.'

'So it isn't just snow and ice that can make the moors and hill roads treacherous,' Luke said soberly.

'What happened that day was a one-off,' she assured him. 'It was just that today's storm took me by surprise, brought it all back, but thankfully I wasn't alone this time and I wasn't out in it.'

'Maybe not,' he agreed grimly, 'but it must have been a harrowing experience.'

She nodded. 'Lightning struck a scarecrow in the field where I was sheltering against the wall, and I thought I was going to be next. So, you see, I've now got this phobia about thunder and lightning.'

'Not without cause,' he told her, and vowed to himself that in future he would do any home visits on the higher levels in bad weather. But they could discuss that another time. Megan was an independent creature and might take some persuading.

He went across to the window and reported, 'There's a break in the clouds and the rain has eased off. We'll soon be able to leave here and get you to where you feel safe.'

You make me feel safe, she wanted to tell him. Wherever you are I want to be. But it wasn't quite that simple. Luke was holding back because of the way she'd told him that, having been married before, he wasn't exactly what she had in mind for a husband.

She knew now that he was *everything* she could want… and more, but would he believe her if she told him that? He was already convinced that the practice was the only thing in her life that she held dear.

As they walked back the way they had come a watery sun had appeared, filtering apologetically across the rain-soaked moorland.

'So much for a quiet Sunday lunch,' Luke said wryly when they stopped outside her cottage. 'That was some storm.'

'And some fuss I made,' Megan said awkwardly. It was the first time she'd spoken since they'd left The Moorend and he'd glanced at her questioningly a few times.

'Forget it,' he said easily. 'We all have our vulnerabilities.' He glanced around him. The sun's appearance had been brief and daylight was fading. 'Are you sure you'll be all right, Megan? We can stay for a while if you want.'

She shook her head and managed a smile. 'I'll be fine, Luke, and thanks for being there for me. I don't usually flip like that.'

'I know. You don't have to explain. Just take care. I'll ring you later this evening to make sure you're all right. OK?'

'Yes,' she told him, and when they'd disappeared from sight she went inside, sank down onto the sofa and let her mind go back to their time in The Moorend during the storm.

Luke had picked up on her panic straight away and taken charge. He'd held her close and calmed her fears, and she knew that was what she wanted more than anything in the world, him holding her, loving her.

But supposing life with Alexis had left such a bad taste behind that he hadn't needed to be told he didn't fit the bill, that he'd no intention of stepping onto the marriage-go-round again?

She was curled up on the sofa half-asleep when he rang, and Luke's first words were ones of apology. 'I'm sorry to be late ringing you, Megan,' he said. 'It's been a bit hectic here. Sue invited Ned to stay for dinner and once that was over I discovered that the boys had a pile of homework they hadn't done and were showing no signs of tackling it. So while she was entertaining Ned I stood over them until they'd finished it, and in the middle of all that Connie rang to say that she's had a phone call to say they're going to operate on her feet next week, so she will be missing from both the surgery and Woodcote House.'

'What about her husband?'

She could tell that he was smiling at the other end of the line as he said, 'I knew that would be the first thing you would ask. He's going into care for a few weeks until she is mobile again. She's not looking forward to any of it, of course, but let's hope the result will make her feel it was worth it.'

He sighed. 'In the midst of all the bedlam at this end I've been envying you the tranquillity of your cottage tucked away on the hillside.'

'I thought you were the man who could live at the side of a coal tip if the company was right,' she teased. 'What's happened to that boast?'

'Nothing. It still stands.'

'Mmm. I see, but getting back to what you said about my peaceful life, remember there's only a fine line between tranquillity and boredom.'

'I'll bear that in mind,' he told her, 'and now, regretfully, I have to go. The first thing I'm going to do in the morning is send off Sonia's blood tests with a request for urgent attention. So I'll see you then, but before I go, have you recovered from this afternoon's trauma?'

'Yes, I'm fine,' she said breezily. 'As you saw, I'll do anything to gain your attention.'

There was a moment's silence and then with his voice deepening he said, 'You have my attention every second, every hour of every day. Goodnight, Megan.'

* * *

The results from Sonia's blood tests were back, showing deficiencies of haemoglobin, vitamin B and folic acid.

'Sounds as if it could be megaloblastic anaemia,' Luke said when he'd read the report.

'So what next?' Megan asked anxiously.

'A bone-marrow biopsy.'

'To check on any large amount of abnormal blood cells?'

'Yes.'

'I'm relieved that it doesn't appear to be what she thought it was,' Megan said thankfully. 'I'll call on her while I'm on my rounds.'

'Yes, do that,' he agreed, 'and I'll arrange the biopsy. And, Megan, be sure to tell her that at this stage it is only what *we* think. The test might show something different, though I doubt it.'

Where she had been slow to notice the portrait when she'd called at the gallery with Luke on the Saturday, its absence was the first thing Megan picked up on as she walked through the door, and when Sonia came through the velvet curtains to greet her she said regretfully, 'You haven't sold the portrait, have you, Sonia?'

'I'm afraid so, my dear.'

'Who did you sell it to? I was going to buy it myself.'

'It was bought by a man who came in yesterday and it immediately caught his eye.'

'I don't believe it,' Megan groaned.

'I know,' Sonia said apologetically. 'It was the best I've ever done and I was reluctant to let it go, but he was really keen to buy it and a customer is a customer. Though if I'd known you wanted it yourself I wouldn't have sold it. Anyway, I'm hoping that isn't what has brought you here this morning. Do you have news of the blood tests?'

Megan nodded. 'Yes. I do. The results show that you might have megaloblastic anaemia.'

'And what might that be?'

'It is a deficiency of three things—haemoglobin, vitamin B and folic acid. All of them can cause that type of anaemia.'

'And so what happens now?'

'Luke is arranging for you to have a bone-marrow biopsy.'

Sonia frowned. 'What might that be?'

'A small sample of bone marrow will be taken from the top of your hip or your breast bone,' Megan explained. 'It will then be examined to see if abnormal cells are present.'

'And if they are?'

'You'll need to improve your diet and will be given a course of vitamin B and folic acid tablets.'

'And that's it!' Sonia exclaimed, her voice thickening. It was the first time she'd shown any emotion. 'I've been an awkward old fool, Meg. I was so sure I had the other thing I didn't look any further. It needed your Dr Anderson to make me see sense.'

Megan hugged Sonia to her. Her friend had lost a lot of weight and was pale and hollow cheeked, but hopefully they were going to be able to do something about that for her. And as for Sonia describing Luke as *her* Dr Anderson, she wished he was.

The attraction between them seemed to have reached stalemate, with neither of them coming out into the open about their feelings. What Luke had said on the phone on Sunday night had seemed like a move in that direction when he'd as good as told her she was never out of his thoughts, but there'd been no follow-up since.

When Megan arrived back at the surgery Luke was still on his rounds and when he came striding in shortly afterwards the first thing he said was, 'How did Sonia react to your news?'

'Like the stoic she is,' she told him. 'Sonia is a strong woman, but she did crumble a little when she thought of how she'd been so sure she had cancer. I just hope that the biopsy proves us right.'

He nodded and before he could comment she said flatly, 'You'll never guess what. Someone came into the gallery yesterday and bought her portrait of me. I can't believe it! I was going to buy it myself.'

'The person must have recognised her talent,' he said easily. 'I remember thinking myself how good it was, though I'm no judge of that sort of thing. Maybe she'll do you another when she's feeling better.'

'I hope so,' was the reply to that, and as she

went to get some lunch he was left hoping that Sonia would keep his secret. That one day when he produced the portrait Megan would understand why he'd bought it.

Winter was settling over the village. At night and in the mornings frost sparkled on the trees and grasses and only melted away when a pale sun appeared.

The spirit of Christmas was in the air now, with the garden centre behind Woodcote House getting ready to attract extra customers and the tickets for the ball at Beresford Lodge selling fast.

The café and Santa's grotto, which were due to be functioning by early December, were taking up their evenings and weekends, with Luke and Ned, a quiet, fair-haired bachelor in his forties, doing the hard work, and Sue and Megan the creative side of the projects, with the occasional suggestion from Owen who was turning out to have an eye for colour.

The grotto was being arranged in the shop area where customers paid for their purchases, and a large conservatory at the back of the house was being transformed into a café.

Amongst the extra work and bustle of the season Sue was too tired each night to do anything other than sleep, and as Megan and Luke watched over her the plan seemed to be working. There was no way they wanted Gareth to be forgotten at Christmas by any of them, least of all by his family, but hopefully it would be with gentle sadness rather than bitter regret.

Sue had asked Megan and Ned to join them on Christmas Day and she'd accepted with pleasure. Her parents were coming over but not until the New Year, and the thought of being with Luke on the most festive day of the year was a joy to look forward to.

Her involvement with the alterations at the garden centre had arisen when he'd said one day as they'd been leaving the practice, 'You remember telling me that tranquillity can soon become boredom? How are you fixed for helping out with the Christmas preparations at the garden center?'

They were together, yet separate, during the day, he thought, and to have Megan around in the evenings would be magical, with no patients or house calls to take her away from him.

He was delighted that Sue had invited her for Christmas Day. It would have been a dull affair without her and he could have seen himself chasing off up the hill to be with her the moment the meal was over and then fretting because he'd deserted Sue on her first Christmas without Gareth.

'I'd love to,' she'd told him, and he'd smiled his pleasure.

Sonia's results from the biopsy had shown what the two doctors had suspected. Because her body wasn't absorbing vitamin B and folic acid, the abnormal cells had appeared. Tests had also shown that the cause wasn't a poor diet, which meant that she would need injections and tablets for the rest of her life to solve the problem.

When they'd told her what the prospects

were, she'd smiled. 'It could have been so much worse, my dears,' she'd told them. 'I owe you a lot, both of you. You, Meg, for worrying about me, and you, Luke, for taking me in hand.' With a twinkle in her eye she added, 'I might even get around to painting your portrait again, my dear.'

'That would be lovely.' Megan had sparkled back at her. 'It will be something for me to look at when I'm old and grey.'

'Get away with you.' Sonia had chuckled and there had been a warm feeling inside her. She'd noticed the way Luke looked at Megan and thought that maybe another portrait wouldn't be necessary.

When Megan called at the post office on her way to the practice on a morning in the middle of November she was dismayed to see a notice on display informing anyone interested that all tickets for the Christmas ball had been sold.

She'd been so busy at the practice during the day and the garden centre in the evenings that it had gone completely out of her mind, and now it was too late. Luke hadn't mentioned it, so either he'd got his ticket or wasn't going because he was too busy, she thought, and felt gloom descending.

She decided that she would ask him when she saw him and then thought better of it. He'd suggested way back when she'd first mentioned it that he should take her, and she'd given him a pert reply instead of being truthful. So maybe he wasn't going to risk a snub again. Much as they enjoyed being in each other's company, she knew that he wasn't going to forget something else she'd said that couldn't have been more offputting. It was up to her to put it right. But how?

To add to her confusion, Sue rang as the day was about to get under way and said, 'Have you time for a quick word?' She sounded flustered and Megan wondered what was amiss.

'Ned has got tickets for the Christmas ball and he's asked me to go with him,' she said awkwardly. 'Do you think I should?'

'I don't see why not,' Megan replied slowly, 'As long as it's what you want.'

'Do you think it's too soon to be seen with someone else? We're just friends, that's all.'

'So why not, then? It's the kind of event where one needs a partner and Gareth wouldn't want you to be sitting at home, moping.'

'Thanks, Meg,' Sue said with a lift to her voice. 'I knew you would sort me out. I'll tell him yes, then.'

When she'd rung off Megan's smile was wry. It looked as if she was the one who was going to be at home, moping. That it was going to be a case of Cinderella would *not* go to the ball.

But the patients in the waiting room would have more serious things than the Christmas ball on their minds and she was there to do what she could to help them. Luke had just arrived and given a cheery wave as he'd gone into his consulting room, so his world seemed to be all right, and Sue's seemed to be improving. Only she seemed to be stuck in a rut.

At her last consultation of the morning, Megan found herself facing a new patient. The man's notes had been transferred from a city

practice to their own and he was there because
of a strained back muscle.

He'd hobbled in, eased himself carefully
onto the chair facing her and said, 'I've hurt
my back, carrying a television set, Doctor. I
moved into the apartment over the antique
shop yesterday and as the friend who was
going to give me a lift didn't turn up, I ended
doing all the heavy lifting myself.' He sighed.
'I'm a maths teacher, due to start at Marley
Ridge Comprehensive School on Monday, and
the last thing I want is to arrive on crutches.'

The man's name was Joel Taylor and his
records said that he was twenty-eight years old.
What they didn't say was that he was attractive
in a husky sort of way, with bright blue eyes
and a shock of fair hair. They didn't need to.
Megan could see that for herself.

'Can you manage to take your shirt off?' she
asked.

He winced. 'I'll try, but it's agony to lift my
arms above my head.'

'Take your time, then,' she advised. It wasn't
policy to help a patient dress or undress as it

could soon be misconstrued, but, watching him struggle, she thought it would be so much quicker if she could help.

He eventually managed it with the occasional groan and when she'd finished examining him she said, 'Everything seems to be in place, but there is some swelling there. I'm going to give you some painkillers and a gel to rub in gently. If it is no better in a couple of days, get back to me.'

'I'll do that,' he said promptly, 'and thank you, Doctor. I can't say it's been a pleasure as my back's killing me. But as I was expecting to be seen by some elderly village type you've been a nice surprise.'

When he was ready to go she walked into Reception with him and was smiling at what he'd just said when Luke came out of his consulting room.

'Who was that?' he asked when Joel Taylor had gone.

'New patient,' she said briefly.

'Really? You seemed to be getting along very well.'

'He seemed like a nice guy.' Without elaborating on that, she added, 'I'm going across to the bakery. Do you want anything?'

'Yes. A smile if you've got any to spare.'

'Sorry. I've used up today's supply,' she told him, still disappointed about the ball.

He shrugged. 'OK. Maybe when you're in a better mood, you'll tell me what's wrong.'

CHAPTER NINE

WHEN Megan arrived at Woodcote House that evening to help put the finishing touches to Santa's grotto, Rebekah was coming down the drive. She still came each day to tidy up and make an evening meal for Sue, Luke and the boys, even though the young widow was now back in charge again. Rebekah's help reduced the stress levels Sue was under, and gave her more time to concentrate on the garden centre.

Connie wasn't around at the moment. Her operation had been a success and she was now mobile again, though walked slowly and painfully. Yet she was happy that she'd gone ahead with it, even though she would have to face the same procedure again soon as only one foot had been operated on so far. It would be some time before she was back working at the surgery and Woodcote House.

When Rebekah saw the young doctor approaching she smiled. The household where she worked was a much happier place these days. Owen and Oliver didn't look so lost. Their mother was gradually facing up to her new responsibilities, and Dr Anderson, who was a tower of strength, was in love with their own Megan. She was sure of it.

While she'd been vacuuming and dusting around the house she'd found a mysterious package hidden away in his bedroom and hadn't been able to resist taking a peek.

It had been a portrait of the young woman now walking towards her, and the fact that it wasn't on view seemed to say that Megan wasn't aware that he'd got it.

'Hi, Rebekah,' Megan said when they drew level. 'Is that another day done and dusted?'

The older woman's smile was still there. 'It is indeed, my dear. I'm going home to put my feet up while you are involved in more work after your busy day at the surgery.'

'I don't mind,' Megan told her. 'It's a different kind of occupation, but just as therapeutic. Are they all in there?'

'Yes. The boys are upstairs, playing computer games. Sue is already at work on the grotto, and the delightful Dr Anderson, who seems to have one eye on the clock for some reason—are you a bit late perhaps?—is fixing the coffee-machine in the café, while Ned concentrates on the plumbing.' With a gentle squeeze of her hand Rebekah went on her way.

When she'd gone Megan stood there without moving. The report on the activity inside the house should have motivated her, but it hadn't. She was aching to have Luke to herself for a little while. Just the two of them without patients and friends around.

At that moment the front door of the house opened and he was there, dressed in old jeans and a T-shirt, with an electric drill in his hand.

He smiled and said easily, 'I thought you weren't coming. What are you standing out here for Meg o' mine?'

Irritated that he should be so carefree while

she was down in the dumps, she thought he'd remembered how Sonia had called her that on the day she'd taken him round to meet her, and said snappily, 'Don't be too quick to make assumptions.' There was nothing she wanted more than to be his. But the likelihood of that happening seemed to be as far away as the moon and stars.

The smile had disappeared, so had the easy manner. His car was parked in the drive and he opened the door on the passenger side and said, 'Get in.'

She wanted to refuse, but suddenly weary she did as he asked, wondering what was coming next. When he'd slotted himself behind the wheel Luke drove off with the drill on the back seat of the car and Megan beside him, thinking that she'd got her wish. She had him to herself, but she hadn't wanted it to be like this.

He pulled up beside the recreation ground at the bottom of the road and came round to open the door for her. There was a bench facing the children's swings and pointing to it he said, 'Sit.'

Once again she obeyed him and when they were seated he turned to her and said, 'So what is the matter, Megan? What have I done?'

'Nothing.'

'Huh! It looks like it.'

She was aware of how childish she was being and all because of the Christmas ball. Yet it wasn't just that, was it? Luke was so near, yet so far all the time. She was head over heels in love. It was a new experience and should have been wonderful, but she was making a mess of everything. But at least she could be truthful. She owed him that.

'I thought you were taking me to the Christmas ball.'

He was staring at her in amazement. 'So that is what it's all about.' He put his hand into one of the back pockets of his jeans and produced two tickets. 'I've got the tickets, but have been holding back in case there were other guys wanting to take you who fitted your requirements better than I do. Like that fellow this morning who, according to his records, is free and unfettered.'

He was quirking a quizzical eyebrow. 'So shall we start again, Megan? Can I take you to the ball?'

'Yes, please,' she said softly as her world righted itself.

'Good.' He was on his feet, holding out his hand, and as he raised her to face him he said, 'For two intelligent people we don't communicate very well in our private lives, do we? You were upset because I hadn't followed up my invitation, and I've been hesitating because I thought you might have had the better offer that you thought you might get when I first asked you.'

'I was just teasing when I said that,' she confessed, so aware of him she felt as if her legs would cave in. He was still holding her hand. It was their only physical contact, yet she felt as if they were melting together. Desire was taking over, spiralling inside her in a warm surge of longing. Her lips were parted, her eyes luminous, and as he looked down at her in the light of the streetlamps Luke thought she was the most beautiful thing he'd ever seen.

He was about to forget all the promises he'd made to himself about giving Megan some space before he told her how he felt when a small voice said, 'Dr. Megan, it's me, Alicia.'

The park had been empty when Luke had taken her in there, and engrossed in each other they hadn't noticed that a family with small children had come in from an entrance at the far end. And now a little hand was pulling at the leg of Megan's jeans.

The two doctors exchanged a smile, and as Luke let Megan's hand fall to her side he took a step back, thinking that little Alicia Adamson had brought them back down to earth and maybe it was as well. For the two of them to be seen in each other's arms in the playground was surely not in keeping with the protocol of the practice. It was going to have to be another time, another place.

Megan had dropped down on to one knee and put her arm around the little girl. 'Hello, Alicia,' she said gently, with a smile for her parents who were some yards away. 'Is your leg better now?'

'Mmm,' the child said, lifting it for her to inspect.

It looked as if it was. Alicia's mother had brought her to the surgery the week before with a nasty sore on her leg. She'd fallen onto an old spade in the garden and gashed it, which had resulted in an infection. Megan had sent her to the nurse to have it treated and she'd been coming in each day to have antiseptic dressings on it, but from the look of it that would no longer be necessary.

As Luke watched her with the little girl there was a lump in his throat. They dealt with children just as much as adults at the practice, but they weren't at the practice now. Yet Megan was just as patient and gentle with Alicia as if they were.

If she would marry him *she* would give him the children he longed for, with red-gold hair and beautiful green eyes, he thought. Yet would she want them to grow up as she had, with parents who were both busy doctors and hadn't much time for family matters? But he didn't want to marry her just for a family. He ached for her, adored her, wished with all his heart he could have met her before Alexis came on the scene.

But he wasn't taking anything for granted. He knew Megan was attracted to him as much as he was to her, but it didn't follow she would marry him if he asked her. She was an idealist and his past didn't meet her requirements.

When the little family had wandered off he said, 'We'd better go before Sue and Ned send out a search party.'

She nodded. The moment she'd been longing for had gone. It hadn't been the right place in any case, she thought wryly. But some joy had come out of it. Luke was taking her to the Christmas ball, and where he thought all these other men who were dying to take her were, she didn't know. In any case, beside him the rest of the eligible male population were as nothing.

'Does it say fancy dress on the tickets?' she asked as he pulled into the drive of Woodcote House once more.

'No. It just stipulates black tie for the men.'

'So I'll have to go shopping, then.'

'I might tag along and let you help me choose my Christmas gifts for Sue and the boys. That's if you don't mind.'

'I don't mind at all,' she told him. 'You can help me to select an evening dress at the same time.'

It was the first week in December and the star attractions at the garden centre were due to open on Saturday with Santa in his grotto, Ned on the door, and Sue and Megan in charge of the café.

They'd been extra-busy at the surgery with coughs and colds, and in the midst of it Aunt Izzy had fallen in the middle of the night and ended up lying on the bedroom floor until morning, when a passer-by had noticed that her curtains had still been drawn and had rung the surgery.

Leaving Luke to deal with her patients, Megan had rushed round to her aunt's house and with the spare key she always kept in her bag had let herself in. Fortunately the old lady hadn't seemed to have broken any bones or developed hyperthermia, as she'd fallen quite close to a radiator, but shock and bruising had prevented her from being able to raise herself upright, and to Megan's dismay her aunt, who had always been in control, seemed to have lost her confidence.

She'd taken her to A and E to be checked over and been told that she'd been lucky, as the only thing she had was heavy bruising, but Izzy didn't want to be on her own at night any more, so until she could find an easier solution Megan was sleeping at her house. Her aunt was all right during the day, but when night came she started to panic. Afraid it might happen again, no matter how much Megan reassured her.

Looking after her patients during the day, helping to get ready for the opening of the new-look garden centre in the evenings, and having disturbed nights with Izzy calling out all the time to make sure she was there, Megan was wishing there were more hours in the day.

As they were leaving the surgery at the end of Friday Luke said, 'You look whacked, Megan, as if you could do with a good night's sleep.'

She gave a tired smile. 'You're not wrong about that.'

'What are you going to do about Izzy?'

'I've spoken to my mother about her. Mum mentioned that there is an apartment for sale next to theirs on the Costa Del Sol, and did I think Aunt Izzy would be interested. Out there they could keep an eye on her, and I know she was rather envious when they made their move.'

'Have you told her what your mother suggested?'

'I haven't, but Mum has, and she says Aunt Izzy seems quite keen, but is worried that she won't be able to sell her house.'

'Are you kidding? It's the nicest house in the village. A dream of a place. If she decides to go, I'll buy it.'

'So you intend to stay,' she breathed as her tiredness fell away.

He was observing her with raised brows. 'Yes, of course. I can't remember ever having said otherwise. There is nothing for me outside this place. All I care about is here. So don't forget. Megan, if your aunt decides to sell, make sure she knows that she has an on-the-spot buyer.'

Oh, she would let Aunt Izzy know that, Megan thought as she drove home in the dark December night. There was nothing surer. Luke had been right when he'd described her house as the nicest in the village. It was a lovely, unspoilt country home, with a large, safe, garden for children to play in, and with a few touches of their own it would be perfect.

But she was getting carried away. So far there was no indication that she would be part of the package if Luke bought her aunt's house. He cared about her, she knew that. But he cared about Sue and the boys, too, and maybe that was how he felt about her, protective and concerned.

If that *was* the case, she supposed she should be grateful, but she wanted more than that. She wanted passion from him, the same kind of desire that made her feel weak whenever she was near him.

Sometimes when she lay alone at night, gazing up at the beams of the old ceiling above her head, she imagined what it would be like if they made love, and if she'd been sleepless before, that really brought her wide awake. She longed for his touch, his lean nakedness next to hers, and most of all to hear him say, *I love you.*

When she arrived at her aunt's house later that evening the old lady said, 'I've made up my mind. I'm going to go out there to be near your mother and father. I shall call the estate agent tomorrow and put my house on the market.'

'Aren't you being a bit hasty?' Megan said slowly. 'There's nothing to say that what occurred a few nights ago will happen again.'

'No. I've made up my mind, and you know that when I do that I don't change it. I feel quite excited about the whole thing. Just as long as I can find a buyer for this place.'

'You've got one. If you are sure you want to sell, Luke will buy it. Why not get the house valued tomorrow and take it from there? He's really keen and won't let you down.'

Izzy was perking up by the minute. 'Wonderful!' she cried. 'I can't think of anyone I would like to live here more, unless it was you.' She gave a knowing smile. 'And what are the chances of that, my dear?'

'Remote at the moment,' she was told.

The garden centre was packed from the moment of opening the following day, and as Megan served coffee, cakes and tasty snacks in the revamped conservatory with Sue by her side, the two friends exchanged smiles.

Ned had just been in to say that Santa Claus was a huge success and why didn't she go and have a peep? There was a long queue of parents with children and as Luke lifted the little ones onto his knee and talked to them, Megan hoped he wasn't thinking about what Alexis had done to him.

When he looked up and their glances met it seemed as if he wasn't. There was content-ment in his expression, the look of a man who had survived the rapids and found himself in calmer waters.

He came into the café for a quick lunch in the early afternoon and as she served him he said,

'Did you tell your aunt I'll buy her house if she decides to sell?'

'Yes, I did. She's already made up her mind to join Mum and Dad and will sell it to you with pleasure. Aunt Izzy is going to have it valued at the first opportunity.'

He reached across, swung her off her feet and danced around with her in his arms. 'That's wonderful, Megan. A place of my own at last! It will be paradise, living there.'

As she stiffened in his arms a voice called, 'You've got a queue, Santa,' and, putting her down carefully he hurried back to the grotto, leaving her to digest the fact that he wanted her aunt's house as a place of his own. She didn't come into the equation.

When she went back behind the counter Sue said, 'What was all that about?'

'My Aunt Izzy has decided to go and live abroad to be near Mum and Dad and Luke is going to buy her house. I suppose he thinks that you're coping brilliantly, and in any case he won't be far away if you need him.'

Sue was looking uncomfortable. Her colour

had risen. 'I hope he isn't moving out because of Ned and I. We *are* more than friends, Megan. I didn't tell you the truth the other day when I asked you about going to the ball with him. He's asked me to marry him and I've said yes.'

'I see,' Megan said slowly. 'Does Luke know?'

'No. Not yet. Ned only asked me an hour ago. I know what people will say, but he is the one person that Gareth would trust to look after us—apart from Luke, that is.'

'And the boys. Have you told them?'

'Yes. I went to find them straight away before they heard it from anyone else.'

'And?'

'They don't mind. They like Ned. Have known him since they were so high.'

'Then go ahead,' Megan told her gently 'It's your life and Ned will make a great husband and stepfather.'

What is the matter with me? Megan thought as the day wore on. Sue had been the indecisive one, the one who needed looking after, but not any more. While she, Megan, had been pussy-footing about, her friend had found happiness again in the form of a new husband.

Ned hadn't let Sue's past affect him. He obviously loved her and that was all that mattered. While she, Miss Choosy, must have hurt Luke a lot when she'd said she didn't want to marry a man who'd been married before. Even if there had been no blame attached to him in the break-up.

By the time the garden centre closed at six o'clock Megan was both mentally and physically exhausted, and as soon as the café had been tidied, ready for the following day, she slipped out while no one was looking and drove home.

When she arrived at the cottage she switched off the engine and, instead of getting out of the car, laid her head on folded arms on the steering-wheel.

It had been a funny day, she thought tiredly. On the good side there'd been the pleasure of seeing all their hard work paying off at the garden centre.

Of a more depressing nature had been Luke's delight at the thought of a place of his own.

Not that she begrudged him that, far from it. He had unselfishly gone the extra mile for Sue and the boys, and that thought led to another. As far as she knew, his sister hadn't yet told him of her wedding plans. He would have mentioned it if she had. She wondered what he would think when he found out. Would he be relieved, or not surprised, as he'd seen more of Sue and Ned together than she had, or would he be dismayed that Sue was marrying again after such a short time?

Her own feelings regarding that were a mixture of emotions. She was glad for Sue, Ned and the boys, and happy that Sue was to marry someone she knew and trusted. But it made her, Megan, feel that she was standing still. She was envious, and ashamed to be so. But it was her own fault.

A man that she'd had a youthful passion for had come back into her life, and she was so in love with him she couldn't think straight. Where was he now? she wondered. Cracking a bottle of champagne to toast the lovers?

Luke would be the obvious person to give his sister away. She just hoped that Sue wouldn't ask her to be a bridesmaid. Her eyelids were drooping and sleep was creeping over her in the warmth of the car.

When he found that Megan had gone Luke was all set to follow her, but Sue waylaid him. She said she had something to tell him, and as he listened gravely to what she had to say he asked the same question that Megan had asked.

'What about Owen and Oliver? Have you told them?'

'Yes. That was one of the first things Megan asked,' she told him.

'So you've told her.'

'Yes, and the boys are happy about it. As I told Meg, they've known Ned since they were little tots. It isn't like them having to get used to a stranger.'

He nodded. 'That's true. Just as long as you're sure that you want to do this.'

'I am. I'm not like Meg, in control of my own life. I need someone to lean on, as you know only too well, and Ned makes me so happy.'

'And so when is the wedding to be?'

'Soon. We aren't sure when.'

He wanted to be with Megan, he thought and wondered why she'd gone in such a rush. He was keen to know what she thought about Sue's news, and he wanted to make sure she was all right. She'd had a gruelling week.

As he drove up the lane to the cottage he saw that her car was parked in front with the headlight still on, but there were no lights on inside the building, So where was she? he wondered. Surely not still in the car?

He had his answer when he bent to look inside and saw her draped over the steering-wheel, asleep. His expression softened. She'd been too exhausted to get out of the car. He was glad he'd followed her home. She might have been asleep for hours if he hadn't turned up.

He tried the door on the driver's side. It wasn't locked and he frowned. It was obvious that she must have fallen asleep almost as soon as she'd stopped the car, which might be all very well on a well-lit driveway, with other properties nearby, but this was crazy. She was alone up there and for the first time he questioned the safety of it.

Under normal circumstances she was cool and capable, quite able to look after herself, but not tonight. She looked vulnerable and pale in the light of a winter moon.

He shook her gently, but she didn't move. He tried again. This time she lifted her head slowly and observed him drowsily.

'What's wrong?' she asked. 'What are you doing here, Luke?'

'I came to find out why you'd left in such a hurry and I discovered you out here fast asleep with the car unlocked.' His anxiety was making him sound censorious but he couldn't help it.

She was straightening up, still drowsy. 'No one comes along here, except me and old Jonas, who has the cottage further along the lane.'

'So that makes it all right to sleep out here, does it?'

She swung her legs out of the car and rose to

stand beside him, and without answering the question said, 'So now you see that I'm all right, don't let me keep you.'

'I am not going anywhere until I've seen you safely inside. And we need to talk.'

'What about?'

'You taking a few days away from the practice and the garden centre to recharge your batteries, for one thing. Your tiredness could mean that you're sickening for something and, as I see it, I'm the only one available to look after you in the present situation.'

'And from the tone of your voice you find it a chore,' she said snappily. 'But tell me, what *is* the present situation? You moving into Aunt Izzy's house? Sue marrying Ned Fairley? Neither of those things are connected with me, are they?'

'Not if you don't want them to be,' he told her grimly, dismayed at the way the conversation was going. When he'd found her asleep in the car he'd wanted to pick her up, carry her inside, tuck her up in bed and watch over her until she woke up.

Instead, they were bickering outside in the

cold night, and as Megan fumbled in her pocket for the door key he said in a gentler tone, 'I'm going to put the kettle on and make us some tea, and then perhaps we might get back to being friends instead of enemies.'

She was being obnoxious and knew it, Megan thought as he put a steaming mug of tea into her hands a little later. It had been stupid to fall asleep in the car with the doors unlocked, and she should be grateful that Luke had taken the time to follow her home.

She'd closed her eyes for a second in the middle of going over the day's events and tiredness had taken over.

'So what do you think of Sue marrying Ned Fairley?' she asked, her glance guarded above the rim of the mug.

'As long as she is absolutely sure it's what she wants to do, it's fine by me,' he said levelly. 'I've seen it coming. Maybe I'm a bit surprised that their feelings are out in the open so soon, but there is really no need to wait, is there?'

'No. I suppose not,' she agreed, thinking that the day *their* feelings were out in the open looked as if it was going to be a long time coming. 'Sue gave her reason for marrying again so soon as her needing someone to lean on, and I understand that. She seemed to think that I didn't have those kind of needs.'

There was a moment's silence in the small sitting room of the cottage and then he asked, 'Do you?'

'Yes. I'm no different to anyone else. I want to marry the man of my dreams one day.'

He was getting to his feet, his face expressionless as he towered above her. 'Well, I'm sure he's out there somewhere.' Before she could reply he left, striding purposefully out into the night, leaving her to face her uncertainties alone.

When she arrived at her aunt's house later in the evening Isabel was having her bedtime cocoa and she said, 'I was beginning to think you weren't coming.'

Megan bent to kiss her worried brow. 'You know I won't let you down, Aunt Izzy. How have you been today?'

'Fine, until I think of going to bed, and then my nerves start playing me up. You can tell your doctor friend that I've had the place valued today and he can come round as soon as he likes to discuss the sale.'

The elderly lady sipped her cocoa. 'When your mother and father come at New Year I'm going to go back with them. They've invited me to stay with them until the deal over the Spanish property is complete. So unless Dr Anderson changes his mind, everything looks like it's going to plan.'

'Luke won't change his mind,' Megan told her. 'He's really looking forward to having a place of his own.' I can vouch for that, she thought glumly.

When she arrived at Woodcote House the next morning Owen and Oliver were on the point of going to meet their friends at the recreation ground, but they stopped when they saw her. Oliver, always the spokesman, asked, 'Did you know that Mum is going to marry Ned, Dr Marshall?'

'Yes, so I believe,' she said without further comment, feeling that if there was anything more to be said it should come from them.

'We're not bothered,' Owen said with a downcast expression. 'We like Ned, but we don't want Uncle Luke to go. He's been great.'

'Your uncle might feel he should move out once your mum marries Ned,' she told them, 'but he's not going to be leaving the village. He'll be living just around the corner.'

'Didn't I tell you, Owen?' Oliver whooped. 'I said he wouldn't leave us.' And with the only cloud on their horizon having been removed, they sauntered off to meet their friends.

As she watched them go a voice said from behind, 'What was all that about?' When she turned, Luke was there.

'The boys were worried that they wouldn't be seeing you any more, but they're fine now I've explained that you'll be living close by. I should have thought you would have put their minds at rest regarding that.'

'I might have done if I'd seen them. They were out all yesterday, and then went straight to a friend's for a sleepover. I didn't know they were back until a moment ago. So you see…'

'Yes, I do,' she told him contritely, 'and I'm sorry for butting into your affairs.'

'It's OK,' he said easily, as if their exchange of words the night before hadn't taken place. 'And what about my suggestion that you stay at home today?'

'I can't leave Sue to run the café on her own,' she protested. 'And in any case, I feel much more rested this morning. Aunt Izzy slept the night through, which meant that so did I. So there's no need to be concerned about me.'

CHAPTER TEN

SONIA was one of those waiting to see Luke on Monday morning. She'd just arrived back from a fortnight in Greece with her friend Barbara, and after some winter sun and a few weeks of Vitamin B injections and folic acid tablets, she was looking much less gaunt.

'And so how are you feeling, Sonia?' he asked her.

'So much better I can hardly believe it,' she said brightly.

'Good. Megan will be pleased to hear that. Has she seen you since you got back?'

'Yes, she called in last night on her way to her Aunt Izzy's. She's sleeping there at present, I believe.' Sonia was observing him questioningly. 'Have you told her that you've bought her portrait yet? Meg was miffed to find it had been sold so quickly, as she wanted it for herself.'

He shook his head. 'No, not yet. The moment never seems right But I'm hoping the time will come. I'm involved in buying her aunt's house and the portrait will hang perfectly in the sitting room there. You'll still keep my secret, won't you?'

'Yes, of course, but try not to be too long. I'm not the world's most patient person.'

When she'd gone to the nurse's room to have a fresh set of blood tests taken, Luke thought wryly that patience was the name of the game. But the first move had to come from Megan, or always at the back of his mind would be the thought that he'd persuaded her to marry him against her better judgement.

They went late-night Christmas shopping on the Wednesday of that same week. With their weekends taken up at the garden centre and the practice to keep them occupied during the day, it was going to be their only opportunity, and the ball was on the coming Friday.

As they drove into the town Luke said, 'So which do we do first, eat or shop?'

'Shop, I think. They usually close about eight, which only gives us a couple of hours. Do you know what you're going to buy for Sue and the boys?'

'Hmm, I think so. Jewellery for my sister, and the latest strip of the football team they support for Owen and Oliver.'

Sitting beside him Megan laughed. 'You make it sound so easy. Wait until we get into the dress departments of the stores.'

That part of it *was* easy, he thought. It was what was going to be his Christmas gift to the woman beside him that had him not thinking straight. She'd asked him to help her choose a dress. That could be his gift to her, but he wondered if she was aware that the request had a certain sort of intimacy about it. That a woman might only ask it of the man in her life, and he had a few doubts on that score.

While he shopped for Sue and the boys Megan bought gifts for her parents, Aunt Izzy and Sonia, and when they met up again she reminded Luke that they had to organise gifts for the staff at the practice.

'Not now, I hope,' he said as he looked around him. Everywhere they'd been had been thronged with shoppers. 'I've been meaning to ask you about that. What is the procedure at the surgery at Christmas?'

'We buy everyone the same gift, wine and chocolates, and have a celebratory drink and mince pies in the early afternoon of Christmas Eve before we close for the holiday. But we don't have to shop for any of that. We have it delivered and the presents are already gift-wrapped.'

'Good,' he said as they went up the escalator taking them to designer labels and less expensive clothes for women. As they stepped off onto thick carpeting he said, 'Have you any idea what you want?'

'Not exactly, but I'll know when I see it,' she told him, letting the pleasure of having him with her on such an occasion wash over her. 'There are some shades I just can't wear with my colouring, like red, purple, some shades of blue, to name a few, so I usually go for green, cream or brown, and sometimes the occasional little black number.'

As she looked along the rails Luke sat and watched her. It was forty minutes to closing time. Would Megan have made a purchase by then? If she was anything like Alexis, she wouldn't have, and that would have been with all the assistants dancing attendance on her.

She turned at that moment and held up two dresses for him to see, an off-the-shoulder cream evening dress and a black one with a plunging neckline and long sleeves. When he smiled his approval she disappeared into the cubicle.

Seconds later there was an announcement over the store's public-address system. A voice was telling customers in measured tones that there was an emergency. Would everyone, please, leave the store in an orderly fashion by the staircases, as the lifts and escalators were not functioning.

Then the lights went out and there was only emergency lighting to see by, and as Megan

swished back the curtains of the cubicle, re-
splendent in the cream dress, there was a mad
rush for the staircases as someone shouted,
'The store's on fire!'

That had everyone moving. She turned back
to take the dress off but Luke said, 'Leave it,
Megan. There's smoke coming up from below.
We need to get moving.'

She nodded and picked up her bag, ready
to join the jostling throng heading for the
stairs, but it wasn't going to be that simple.
A young mother with a baby in a buggy and
two other young children was standing panic-
stricken beside them. Stopping, they each
swung a child up into their arms and
followed the crowd.

It was like being swept along by the tide as
they reached the stairs. The mother had left the
buggy behind and was carrying the baby in her
arms. Megan told her to go first, then followed
close behind. When she turned to see where
Luke was she couldn't find him at first and
then she picked him out some way back with
the child in one arm and the other protectively

around the shoulders of an old man who was wheezing from the smoke.

Then mercifully they were at ground level and the doors were open for them to stagger out into the fresh air with the clang of fire engines in their ears. But when she turned Luke wasn't behind them.

Passing the child she'd been carrying back to its mother, she went back inside, scanning the faces of the downward-moving crowd for any sign of him.

A teenage lad had come into view, carrying the other child that Luke had picked up, and the old man was being assisted by someone else.

'Where's the man who passed the child to you?' she asked urgently of the youth when he drew level.

'You mean the doctor fellow?' he gasped. 'He went back. There were flames coming up around the escalator and some people had collapsed from the smoke. When he found out, he fought his way back to see what he could do.'

'Move along, madam. You're blocking the way,' an official-sounding voice said at her elbow, and she turned to find a policeman there.

'I'm a doctor,' she cried. 'We are both doctors, but my colleague has gone back to help those still inside. I need to go to him.'

'I'm afraid not,' he told her decisively. 'The fire service are here and will get to him as quickly as possible. They're putting their ladders up as the staircases are still full of people.'

'What caused the fire?' somebody shouted from the street outside.

'We believe it is an electrical fault confined to the first and second floors, but it hasn't been confirmed yet,' he told them. To Megan he said in an even more decisive tone, 'Will you, please, clear the way for those who are still evacuating the building, madam?'

She nodded mutely. They'd been so happy, the two of them in each other's company. Making no demands of each other. Sauntering around the shops at peace with the world, and they'd walked into a nightmare.

She didn't question why Luke had gone back. It would have been as natural as breathing for him to do so, as it would have been for herself if she'd been given the chance. But supposing she lost him and had never told him how much she cared?

The mother of the children had appeared at her side and with her bewildered brood looking on she said, 'Thank you. I don't know how I would have managed without you and your husband. They say he's gone back in. That is some man you have there. He's so brave.'

There was no point in explaining to this stranger that Luke wasn't her husband, Megan thought, but, oh, how she wished he was. If he didn't propose, she would, and as flames began to lick around the windows on the second floor, where they'd been when the announcement was made, she thought despairingly that she might not get the chance.

A paramedic, waiting nearby for casualties to be brought out into the cold December night, had wrapped a blanket around her shoulders as she was still wearing the evening dress she'd been trying on, and she managed a tearful word of thanks.

'They're bringing them out now,' he said.

'The fire chief has just said that the fire is under control and the building has been cleared. So your man should be coming out shortly.'

Would he, though, she thought desperately, and what state would he be in? Supposing it had been too late and Luke had gone for ever? They'd brought six people out and he wasn't any of them, so where was he? She scanned the scene frantically.

It was at that moment that she heard his voice calling her name and her heart stood still. He was coming out of the store all in one piece, eyes red-rimmed, teeth shining whitely in a smoke blackened face. He was the most welcome sight she'd ever seen.

As she flew into his arms she was weeping out her thankfulness in great gulping sobs and he said gently. 'I had to go back, Megan.'

'Yes, I know you did,' she choked, 'but I thought I was never going to see you again and I'd never told you how much you mean to me.'

As she was about to pour out her heart to him he said, 'So now you don't have to worry. I'm here, safe and sound.'

She flinched. How could he be so casual? She'd been expecting this to be the moment when they opened their hearts to each other, but it seemed as if Luke had nothing to say.

The paramedic who'd given her the blanket was hovering and as she backed away he said, 'I think you should come back to A and E to be checked over, sir. You were up there in the smoke for quite a while and I see you have a burn on your hand.'

'Yes, sure,' he agreed, adding to Megan, 'Will you drive the car back home for me, please? It's insured for any driver.'

'If you don't want me with you, yes,' she told him, stiffly, wondering if he had any idea of what she'd gone through during those moments outside the store.

Six people had been taken to hospital suffering from smoke inhalation and minor burns, and one of those that Luke had gone back to help had suffered a mild heart attack. But because the building had been evacuated sensibly no one had been crushed on the staircases, often the cause of the most casualties on such occasions.

He was taking off the leather jacket he'd worn for their outing. 'Here, put this on, Megan,' he said, 'before you get frostbite in that dress. It smells a bit smoky but it will keep you warm.' And before she could argue he stepped into the ambulance and was whisked away.

When she put the jacket on she could still feel the warmth of him inside it, and as she hugged its loose folds around her she thought bleakly that it had been some night, with a grand finale of Luke cutting her short as she'd been about to confess her love for him.

Thank goodness he'd stopped the outpouring of her feelings before she'd made a complete fool of herself, and, conscious that she must look somewhat quaint in a long evening dress and a man's jacket that was far too big for her, she made her way to where they'd parked the car.

She hadn't been back at the cottage long when Luke phoned to check that she'd arrived home safely. 'I've had the burn on my hand dressed,' he told her. 'I got it from touching the side of the escalator. It was red-hot. They don't seem to have any worries about my breathing. So I'm allowed home and am at present waiting for a taxi. Sleep tight, Megan, and don't worry about a thing. I'll pick my car up in the morning.'

Sleep tight? she thought when he'd gone off the line. Did he have to be so casual about the night's events? But maybe casual was how he saw their relationship, and if that was what Luke wanted, he could have it, she thought angrily.

As he waited for the taxi outside A and E, Luke was thinking sombrely that if it took a trauma like tonight's to make Megan feel she had to admit she cared for him, he didn't want to know. It would have been so easy to take advantage of her fear and distress, but when she'd calmed down would she have regretted what she'd said?

If ever she became his, it would be when she was thinking clearly, not in a highly emotional state, and if that was going to tax his patience to the limit, it was how it was going to have to be.

* * *

When Luke went to pick up the car the following morning Megan looked as if she hadn't been up long. She was still in her nightdress with a robe slung over it, and the bright halo of her hair was tousled from a miserable wakeful night when she opened the door to him with an expression that said if she looked a mess, so what?

There was a parcel on a chair near the door and she said, 'I've been packing up the dress from last night, ready for it to go back to the store.'

He nodded. 'We never did get our shopping finished, did we? What happened to the things we'd already bought?'

'They got left behind in the chaos, but there are still two weeks to Christmas, and I'll wear something I've already got to the ball.'

'Are you sure? We can have another try.'

'Yes. I'm sure,' she said in clipped tones. 'It would have been an extravagance in any case.'

'You seem to have changed your mind on that. I thought you wanted it because it was going to be a special night.'

'That might have been the case, but things change, don't they?'

'Only if we want them to,' he said smoothly. 'And are you intending turning up at the surgery? It's only twenty minutes to starting time.'

'Yes, of course I am. *If* you'll stop delaying me,' she told him in the same tone.

'Only I did suggest that you take a few days off if you remember.'

'I don't need time off. The practice will always be my first concern.'

'Fair enough,' he said levelly. 'I'll see you there.' His glance was on her night attire. 'At whatever time you arrive.'

When Luke had gone Megan had a quick shower, brushed the tangles out of her hair, flung on one of the suits she wore for the surgery and set off down the hill, arriving triumphantly on the practice forecourt at exactly half past eight.

Unable to resist making the point, she posed in the doorway of Luke's consulting room for it to register. He looked up from the paperwork in front of him and said, 'A very praiseworthy effort. Except for the odd shoes.'

She looked down at her feet and, sure enough, one shoe was black and the other brown. 'I have a spare pair in the cupboard at the back of Reception,' she told him unruffled, and went to start her day.

When she'd gone Luke gazed after her bleakly. He knew he'd upset her, and regretted being so abrupt when she'd been about to pour her heart out to him the previous night. He owed her an apology, but what to say without making things worse?

For weeks he'd been carrying around the ring that he ached to see on her finger. A solitaire green diamond to match her eyes, that would tell the world that she was his. But it wasn't going to see the light of day if he carried on like this.

Yet he was so wary of making another mistake. If he proposed to her and she said yes, the rest of his days on earth would be enchantment. If she said no, for the reason she'd once spelt out for him, he would stay on his own forever. Maybe he'd held back long enough and it was time to make a move.

His sister and Ned weren't letting the grass grow under their feet, but Sue didn't have the same sort of track record as he had. They were talking of a wedding in the New Year and much as he wanted Sue to be happy, he groaned at the thought of taking part when his own dreams were so unfulfilled.

John Meadowcroft, an elderly farmer, was one of those waiting to see him when the morning surgery got under way, and as he listened to what he had to say Luke started to think that here could be a case of the debilitating Parkinson's disease.

'My right hand keeps trembling,' the big, bluff farmer told him. 'It's all right while I'm using it, but it starts when it's at rest.'

'Any other symptoms?' Luke asked, with a smile for the most well-known sheep farmer in the area.

'It's difficult to tell when old age is creeping on. Sometimes I feel quite stiff. Other times I feel weak, which is not me. I've always been as strong as a horse, but not any more. The wife and I have been wondering about Parkinson's.'

'Let's not jump to any conclusions yet. But I'm going to send you to a doctor who specialises in the treatment of Parkinson's disease and we'll see what he comes up with. And be assured, Mr Meadowcroft, if you are suffering from the onset of it, there are new procedures in medicine that will make your quality of life much better than it would have been some years ago. Patients diagnosed with it are usually started on Levodopa, which helps control the progress of the illness. But first let's see what the consultant has to say.'

As he got up to go the farmer said, 'How are you settling into village life, Doctor?'

Luke smiled. 'I love it.'

'Aye. It would be a strange 'un that didn't. Are we going to see you at the ball?' John asked.

'Yes, you are. I'm really looking forward to it.' In more ways than one, he thought.

'The wife and meself are the MCs for the

night. We're very much into ballroom dancing *and* jive when we're not working on the farm. But I won't be doing much of that if I've got Parkinson's, will I?'

'Like I said, let's not jump to conclusions,' Luke said. 'You could have many years of dancing ahead of you, even if it is the case.'

'Let's hope so,' John said.

That evening Megan went through her wardrobe and couldn't find anything she wanted to wear at the ball the following night. The package containing the cream dress was still waiting to be posted and on impulse she took it out of the wrapping and tried it on again. She'd had it dry-cleaned, even though the smoke luckily hadn't marked it, and it looked perfect.

She'd felt in the store that it was just what she wanted, and it still was. If she phoned the store in the morning and explained that she'd left the premises in one of their dresses and would like to keep it, she felt certain that, having already missed the item, they would be only too pleased for her to pay by credit card over the phone and then her problem of what to wear would be solved.

With that settled she set off to spend the night at Aunt Izzy's once more, and wondered what arrangement they could make for the following night when she would be late back from the ball.

'Rebekah has offered to stay tomorrow night,' Isabel told her when she arrived, putting her concerns to rest. 'So you won't have to do a Cinderella.'

Megan's smile was wry. She'd found the prince. There were no ugly sisters to vent their spite, but she wasn't jumping for joy. It would be another occasion when she and Luke were still hedging with each other, and after the other night *she* would be playing it very cool.

'Did you know that John Meadowcroft and his wife are the MCs tonight?' he said on Friday morning.

Megan observed him without surprise. 'No, I didn't. They go in for a lot of competitions, so I suppose they're the obvious choice. When did you see John?'

'He came to consult me yesterday. I hope I'm wrong, but I'm pretty sure he's starting with Parkinson's.'

'Oh, no!'

'Oh, yes, I'm afraid. I've seen too much of it not to recognise it, but we need to be sure. Anyway, have you sorted out what you're wearing yet?'

'Yes. I think so.' She had yet to ring the store.

'So what time shall I pick you up?'

'What time does it start?'

'The meal is at seven-thirty.'

'Sevenish, then, if that's all right with you. What has Sue arranged about the boys?'

'They've conveniently got a sleepover. So seven it is. And before we go to our separate rooms, are you still angry with me?'

'Er, maybe disillusioned is a better word.'

'Whatever. The main thing is you are not happy.'

'I'm all right,' she told him dismissively, and went to face her patients, wondering what all that had been about. They were talking in riddles again.

* * *

As the day progressed winter was really making its presence felt. There had been warnings of snow and strong winds, which in the extreme spelt blizzard conditions. Knowing the tops like she did, Megan was hoping that anyone living up there wouldn't be prevented from joining the festive crowd at Beresford Lodge.

It included herself, as once snow started to fall it was amazing how quickly roads were cut off, and with the addition of strong winds it would drift, making driving dangerous and difficult.

The surgery had been reasonably quiet. It was beginning to look as if they would manage an early finish and Luke said, 'Why don't you get off while the roads are reasonable, Megan? Take your things to Sue's place and get changed there. If the cottage gets snowed in, you'll be stuck there and won't make it to the ball.'

She sighed. This wasn't how she'd wanted it to be. She'd planned on opening the door to Luke when he came for her, looking cool and elegant. Instead, he would be around while she was getting ready and it wouldn't be the same.

But there was unmistakable logic in what he was suggesting. She knew the caprices of the weather up on the tops as well as anyone, certainly more than Luke did, so she nodded and reluctantly made a quick departure.

It wasn't as bad as she'd expected when she turned onto the hill road, until she came to the lane where she lived, and as she drove up to the cottage her eyes widened. Old Jonas, her neighbour, was lying on the pavement outside her cottage with one of his legs twisted awkwardly beneath him.

'Megan!' he gasped through blue lips as she stopped the car beside him. 'I slipped and I think I've broken me leg.'

'How long have you been lying here?' she asked anxiously in the fading light.

'I don't know, but it seems a long time.'

She bent and examined the angle of his leg. 'It does look like a fracture. I can't risk moving you in case I do more damage,' she told him. 'I hope I can get a signal on my phone in this dreadful weather to get an ambulance up here.'

The fates were with her. She got through to the emergency services and made her request, telling them that it was extremely urgent before the old man froze to death. Then she ran inside, grabbed blankets and filled hot-water bottles wrapped in towels, to place on top of him until help came.

Jonas was a tough old guy, she thought as she monitored his breathing and pulse, but it wasn't going to be enough to prevent hypothermia if he wasn't moved into the warmth soon.

She'd given him something for the pain and now he seemed to be in a doze, and as she shivered in the cold Megan prayed the ambulance would arrive before the weather closed in on them.

It did. She could hear its siren as it came up the hill and then its headlights were lighting up the dark lane, with the snow swirling around them.

The paramedics lifted Jonas carefully onto a stretcher, making sure that the injured leg was kept in position, and then covered him in foil to fight the cold.

'Don't worry about me, lass,' Jonas told her weakly, 'but I'd be obliged if you'd see to my cat.'

'Yes, of course I will,' she told him with a warm smile. 'I'll be in to see you the first chance I get.'

Then the ambulance was speeding off into the night and she was left to gather her wits.

The first thing she did once inside the cottage was to try to get Luke on her mobile phone. But this time there was no signal and she groaned. It had been ages since she'd left the practice. He would be wondering where she was, why she hadn't turned up at Sue's house, and there was nothing she could do about it except try to get back down the hill…

Without wasting a second, she packed a small case with the dress, underwear, shoes and the make-up she was going to need, and opened the door once more to the atrocious weather.

She shuddered and took a step back as her dread of storms came galloping back and it was then that she saw him coming along the lane on foot, battling against the wind and the snow, and she almost wept with relief.

But it was not to be a blissful moment. As he came up the path he bellowed, 'What on earth have you been doing all this time, Megan? Have you seen the weather?'

'Of course I've seen the weather,' she cried. 'I could hardly miss it, could I? I've been looking after Jonas, my neighbour. I found him almost on my doorstep with what I'm expecting to be a broken leg. I couldn't risk moving him so I've been sitting there beside him, trying to keep hypothermia at bay, while we waited for an ambulance.'

'I've been frantic,' he said tightly as she stepped back to let him in.

'Imagining you up here alone and being afraid of the storm as you were that other time, or you having set off and been stuck in a drift somewhere.'

'Frantic was how I felt the other night when you were inside that burning building,' she told him angrily, 'but you didn't seem to be bothered. Wouldn't let me say what I wanted to say, which was that I love and adore you. Can't get you out of my mind. I was half in love with you when I sent the Valentine card, but that was nothing to what I feel now. I know I upset you when I said I would want to be the first love of the man I married, but it wasn't meant to be a criticism of you personally and I've regretted saying it ever since.'

Luke was peeling off his wet jacket, revealing his dinner suit beneath. 'Oh, Megan,' he said raggedly, 'what are we doing to each other? I can't hold back any longer. It's killing me. You *are* my first love. My feelings for Alexis weren't love. It was a mad infatuation that I allowed to propel me to the altar, and I've had plenty of time to face up to that fact. Apparently I was unique amongst her men friends because I was the only one who ever put a wedding ring on her finger, for what good it did me.'

He held out his arms and said softly, 'Come here, my beautiful, precious girl…my Valentine, and let me show you how much I love you.' And with everything else forgotten that was what he did.

Much later, with the ring sparkling on her

finger, he said, 'How about a St Valentine's Day wedding?'

She smiled up at him from the circle of his arms. 'That would be perfect. We won't be crowding Sue and Ned. They'll have time to get their wedding over, and then it will be our turn. Luke, I still can't believe that you love me as much as I love you.'

'You have to believe it. We have a lifetime of loving to look forward to,' he said tenderly. 'It will be another husband-and-wife team running the practice.'

Megan smiled. 'Only until we start having babies. Then we'll have to find a locum. My parents were always too busy to spend much time with me, and that isn't how it's going to be with our children.'

'Our children,' he breathed. 'Two magical words.'

It was ten o'clock and when Luke went to the door to check on the weather he came back to report that the wind had dropped and that the gritters had been by.

'If they've gritted the lane they'll certainly have done the same to the road down to the village,' she told him. 'Why don't I get changed and we go to the ball? It will be on for hours yet and it would be a shame to miss it, as long as the roads are accessible.'

'Fine by me,' he said softly. 'Though I shall have to restrain myself from going up on to the stage and telling everyone how fortunate I am because the girl of my dreams has said she'll marry me.'

When they entered the ballroom at Beresford Lodge the first thing they saw was John Meadowcroft and his wife doing a lively quick-step around the floor, and the feet that Luke had last seen in heavy boots were moving smoothly along in a pair of shiny, black, patent-leather shoes.

Then they got chatting to Elise and her husband. The results of Elise's amniocentesis had come back normal, and the mother-to-be was glowing with good health and happiness. The whole family were now thrilled that they were to have a new addition, the girls having got used to the idea, and Megan and Luke were delighted that things were going well for them.

Shortly afterwards they joined the dancing themselves and as he looked down at the girl he loved, with smooth shoulders bare above the cream dress and her eyes dreamy with happiness, Luke sent up a prayer of thanks to St Valentine.

Christmas had been and gone. They'd shared it with Sue, Ned and the boys, and there'd been happiness and goodwill all around them, with Gareth not forgotten.

Sue and Ned's wedding had been a quiet affair at the registry office, with Luke to give her away, Megan as bridesmaid and the boys happy enough but casting yearning looks at the recreation ground across the way where their friends were congregated.

Megan's parents had been over for New Year and been delighted to know that Luke was to be their son-in-law. They'd gone back in the first week in January and taken Izzy with them, and the three of them would be returning for the St Valentine's Day wedding, when Izzy would sign the contract that would make Luke the owner of her house.

She'd left a key so that they could do some jobs around the place, and on the night before she was due to arrive Luke had suggested to Megan that they go round there.

'Close your eyes,' he said as he led the way into the sitting room. Puzzled, she did as he asked. 'You can open them now,' he told her, and the first thing she saw when she did was her portrait on the wall.

Tears glistened on her lashes. How could she have ever doubted that he loved her? she thought. Luke had bought the painting months ago, long before she'd sorted her feelings out. She remembered Sonia saying that the purchaser had been very keen to buy it.

'I love you,' she said, moving into his arms.

'Why?' he questioned laughingly. 'Is it because I know a good painting when I see one?'

* * *

On a cold day in February a bride and her new husband, with most of the villagers gathered around them, were on the riverbank.

It hadn't been possible to have the wedding ceremony there, as Megan had once dreamed, so it had taken place in the beautiful old village church. But Luke had ensured that at least a part of his bride's dearest wish was being fulfilled, as they stood on her beloved riverbank in each other's arms and smiled for their first photographs as husband and wife.

MEDICAL™

Large Print

Titles for the next six months…

January

SINGLE DAD, OUTBACK WIFE	Amy Andrews
A WEDDING IN THE VILLAGE	Abigail Gordon
IN HIS ANGEL'S ARMS	Lynne Marshall
THE FRENCH DOCTOR'S MIDWIFE BRIDE	Fiona Lowe
A FATHER FOR HER SON	Rebecca Lang
THE SURGEON'S MARRIAGE PROPOSAL	Molly Evans

February

THE ITALIAN GP'S BRIDE	Kate Hardy
THE CONSULTANT'S ITALIAN KNIGHT	Maggie Kingsley
HER MAN OF HONOUR	Melanie Milburne
ONE SPECIAL NIGHT…	Margaret McDonagh
THE DOCTOR'S PREGNANCY SECRET	Leah Martyn
BRIDE FOR A SINGLE DAD	Laura Iding

March

THE SINGLE DAD'S MARRIAGE WISH	Carol Marinelli
THE PLAYBOY DOCTOR'S PROPOSAL	Alison Roberts
THE CONSULTANT'S SURPRISE CHILD	Joanna Neil
DR FERRERO'S BABY SECRET	Jennifer Taylor
THEIR VERY SPECIAL CHILD	Dianne Drake
THE SURGEON'S RUNAWAY BRIDE	Olivia Gates

MILLS & BOON

Pure reading pleasure

1207 LP 2P P1 Medical

MEDICAL™

Large Print

April

THE ITALIAN COUNT'S BABY — Amy Andrews
THE NURSE HE'S BEEN WAITING FOR — Meredith Webber
HIS LONG-AWAITED BRIDE — Jessica Matthews
A WOMAN TO BELONG TO — Fiona Lowe
WEDDING AT PELICAN BEACH — Emily Forbes
DR CAMPBELL'S SECRET SON — Anne Fraser

May

THE MAGIC OF CHRISTMAS — Sarah Morgan
THEIR LOST-AND-FOUND FAMILY — Marion Lennox
CHRISTMAS BRIDE-TO-BE — Alison Roberts
HIS CHRISTMAS PROPOSAL — Lucy Clark
BABY: FOUND AT CHRISTMAS — Laura Iding
THE DOCTOR'S PREGNANCY BOMBSHELL — Janice Lynn

June

CHRISTMAS EVE BABY — Caroline Anderson
LONG-LOST SON: BRAND-NEW FAMILY — Lilian Darcy
THEIR LITTLE CHRISTMAS MIRACLE — Jennifer Taylor
TWINS FOR A CHRISTMAS BRIDE — Josie Metcalfe
THE DOCTOR'S VERY SPECIAL CHRISTMAS — Kate Hardy
A PREGNANT NURSE'S CHRISTMAS WISH — Meredith Webber

MILLS & BOON®
Pure reading pleasure

1207 LP 2P P2 Medical